man standing,
but can she
make him fall?

WOMANIZER

KATY EVANS

New York Times & *USA Today* Bestselling Author

Copyright © Katy Evans

First paperback edition: December 2016

Cover design by James T. Egan, www.bookflydesign.com
Interior formatting by JT Formatting

10 9 8 7 6 5 4 2 1

Library of Congress Cataloguing-in-Publication Data is available

ISBN-13: 978-1536958751

To all the unplanned things in life

TABLE OF CONTENTS

PLAYLIST

"I Lived" by OneRepublic
"All You Are" by Bluebox
"TiO" by Zayn
"For Your Entertainment" by
Adam Lambert
"Into You" by Ariana Grande
"Lost Stars" by Adam Levine
"Champagne" by Ferras
"Turn the Night Up" by Enrique Iglesias
"Fiction" by Kygo
"You Make the Rain Fall" by
Kevin Rudolf
"Here With Me" by Dido
"Put Your Arms Around Me" by Texas

MOVING TO CHICAGO

I stare out the plane window at Chicago beneath me. My home for the next three months.

My best friends, Farrah and Veronica, didn't believe the news.

They weren't the only ones who didn't believe the news. Nobody in the entire Hill Country believed me, not even my dream employer, Daniel Radisson, head of Radisson Investments in Austin, who refused my application for internship and told me to get some experience somewhere else and come back to him when I was ready. I stopped by to tell him that I'd found a job and I'd be coming back to work for him when I finished.

"You found an internship at the biggest firm in Chicago yourself?" he asked, shaking his head incredulously as he took in my fashionable pumps, miniskirt, cute little sequined top, and cross-body bag.

I blinked at his complete lack of belief in me, resisting the urge to steal my hand around my waist and cross my fingers behind my back as I said a little fib.

I loathed admitting that my brother got the job for me.

I hate lying, so I resisted, but I hate being underestimated more.

My brother may have gotten this job for me, but I'm going to be the one who keeps it and climbs the ranks on my own merit. No favors from anyone anymore. One day I will have my own business and help people realize their own dreams.

"My brother is friends with the CEO, and they were happy to have me on board," I said—which, technically, is true. Tahoe actually only said, *Talked to Carmichael. Send all paperwork to this email. Start first week of June.*

"Happy" wasn't mentioned but if his friend agreed, then I assume he is happy I'm coming on board.

At least *I* am.

I've been underestimated my whole life. For my eighteenth birthday present, my brother sent me to France for the summer and all I came back saying was *oui*. Huge disappointment to my parents, who wanted me to come back a fully sophisticated, French-speaking lady. So I don't pick up foreign languages easily? It's not the end of the world. I have a business degree, and I have big dreams.

So the last week of May, all packed and ready and with one wistful last look at the bedroom I've lived in most of my teenage years and adult life, I take a risk—not only did I leave home, but I actually caved in to my brother's insistence to send his jet to pick me up and fly me to the Windy City.

There were tears when my parents stuffed my luggage into the trunk of the family SUV, and more tears as we reached the airport.

Definitely I was the one most tearful. I'm just an easy person to make cry, don't judge.

It doesn't mean I cannot be badass. Ask Ulysses Harrison, who got punched in the nuts when he tried to feel my boobs just as they started growing.

I hugged my mom and dad, first inhaling my mom's scent of cinnamon and apples, then getting a good whiff of my dad's Old Spice. After begrudgingly letting go, I took the steps leading up to my brother's luxurious private jet. From the top of the stairs, I waved at them, and they waved back, with one arm wrapped around each other and the other waving at me. My dad was smiling and wearing his I'm-tough-but-dammit-I'm-feeling-emotional face. My mom slipped on a pair of shades so I couldn't see if her eyes were still weepy or not.

When the pilot closed the door, I settled in a seat near the plane wings so that I didn't feel as if there was nothing beneath me. A mindfuck, just so I can force myself to fly.

The plane engines geared up, and I leaned back and closed my eyes for the flight, turning the ring on my left hand round and round.

Heights and I . . . let's just say we don't go well.

My brother saved me from heights once, and he's the only one I feel safe with. I wouldn't be caught dead flying commercial. But this is his plane. And when I opened my eyes mid-flight, I saw a message on one of the seats that read, *Just hang in there. It'll be over in a second.*

I laughed, and now I'm seconds away from landing, listening to some music to distract myself, settling for the song "I Lived" on replay as the plane finally lands in Chicago. My home for the next three months and the internship that will be the first step of many, many I need to take to make my career dreams come true.

My brother Tahoe and his girlfriend pick me up at the airport in a very dirty Rolls-Royce Ghost. I swear my brother likes fine things, but he doesn't give a shit about using them until they're done. Me? I'm the sort of girl who stores her favorite purse with filler and in double dust bags and then in a box, rarely using it for fear of scratching it. Tahoe doesn't even care enough to bother to pay someone to clean his $300k car.

We reach a beautiful, tall skyscraper in the Loop, and take the elevator up.

He kisses my cheek after we board.

"Stay out of the clubs, Liv," Tahoe whispers. A warning.

"Leave her alone, you big bully," his girlfriend defends me.

Where my brother is tall and blond and raw, his girlfriend Regina is curvy and dark-haired and sultry.

He pins her at his side and kisses her silent, a big smack that makes her groan as if she doesn't like it. But she flushes, so she obviously does. "I'm her big brother, it's my job not to." He grins down at her with a special look in his eyes he gets only when he looks at her, and then looks at me somberly. "Seriously. Stay out of the clubs."

I groan. "I'm not interested, okay? I came here to *work*. Plus I survived seven years in Texas without you policing my nightly activities."

But the truth is, I love my brother. He's a little rough around the edges but he means well. I love my family and I want them to be proud of me.

"Good. Carmichael's doing this as a personal favor to me," he says as we step out on my floor.

"Thanks for reminding me I don't have qualities of my own to get me an internship."

"In a Fortune 500 company? Sis, you're good . . ."

I frown. "But not that good?"

He looks at me with that smirk of his, then reaches out and rumples my hair. "You're good. Make me proud, okay?" He tips my chin up.

I nod.

Callan Carmichael. I don't know him, even though he's apparently a close friend of my brother. When my brother moved to Chicago and I came to visit, he always told me to stay away from his friends. Now I'm old enough to work at one of their firms—Carma Inc. For the owner and CEO himself. Carma is a conglomerate of ten-plus huge multibillion-dollar companies involving media, real estate, and worldwide investments, and takeovers are Carmichael's specialty. He's a land shark. I'm not into city gossip, much less in a city I didn't live in until an hour ago, but I know that in Chicago they speak of him with a touch of fear in their voice. Carma Inc. has been bringing karma to bad business handling for decades, without mercy.

Well it's time to seize my own karma, and I breathe in as I stop at my apartment door.

I may have agreed to let my brother send his jet, but when he said he was renting me a place in his same building, I set my foot down. This is my independence we're talking about. So we compromised when I couldn't find anything affordable near work.

I'm going to be taking over his girlfriend's lease, since she basically lives with Tahoe now.

Tahoe's friend Will Blackstone has a prime building in the Loop that he's demolishing to make new apartment complexes. The permits are still underway and could take a while, and in the meantime Gina had a great rental at an unbelievable price that was sitting mostly unused. She still has some of her stuff over here, but what she needs, she has at Tahoe's. It'll be my place for the next few months.

And suddenly here I am, filled with a rush of excitement when I use my brand-new key to open my brand-new place for the first time.

"You going to open that door today, little sis?" Tahoe asks, shoulder propped on the wall as he waits not-so-patiently.

"Give me a second! Let me savor this!" I protest.

My hand trembles a little and my brother doesn't miss it, but he still lets me be the one to open the door.

I finally do, stepping inside.

It's a one-bedroom, two-bath apartment with a closet as big as my room in Texas, a huge kitchen for entertaining, a living room with views of the city that are to die for, and hardwood floors that smell delicious.

"Oh, I miss this place," Regina says with a sigh.

Tahoe raises his eyebrows at her.

"I didn't say I liked it more than your place." She nudges him with her toe, and he grins at her.

While they make goo-goo eyes at each other, I go and open the window. Gina sold me on the place when she told me the air smells of chocolate because there's a chocolate factory nearby.

I take a good whiff, and the air not only smells like chocolate, it tastes like it too.

I scan my neighboring buildings and cannot believe I'm really here. I pinch myself a little, and it *stings*. It must be real!

The buildings nearby are beautiful, the streets clean. We make a trip downstairs to bring up all of my luggage.

In the closet, Regina has set her stuff on one side, but even with only half the space available, I can't fill this closet on my own, it's so big.

I hang my clothes and actually—unlike my Texas friends—I really *like* closets that aren't crammed. Someone once told me when you cleaned out your closet it left room for new things to come into your life. Mine always has just enough space to welcome something. What that something is, I don't know. But something.

So Gina helps me unpack, and my brother brings Chinese takeout for us to have a late lunch together, and when they leave to go get ready for some posh dinner they must attend, I look around the space and cannot believe this is my first place on my own.

It feels a little odd not to hear my parents downstairs. But I hear the city sounds outside, of life and bustling activity, and it pleases me.

In the living room, I add just one pillow I brought from home that has a colorful little crown and this embroidered right on top of it:

QUEEN OF EFFING EVERYTHING

My grandmother gave it to me. If there was ever any queen in Texas, she is it.

At eighty-two, she's still the coolest gran I know. My nana is my own Betty White with perfect white hair and more expletives in her dictionary than a sailor will ever know.

The only purchase Gina never got around to making was a set of stools for the kitchen island. Since I want to learn to live on my own salary and plan to avoid superfluous spending, I'll just pull the desk chair with a little cushion over when I need it.

I make my bed and organize the framed photographs of Tahoe, Mom, Dad, and me on my nightstand. Then I huff and puff until I get my suitcases up on the top shelf of the closet so they don't take up any floor space.

That night, I sleep for the first time in my life in a whole apartment just for me.

I'm not that sure I like it.

Yet.

On Sunday, I finish organizing the closet in my new apartment and then add office stuff to my brand-new briefcase—a gift from my proud parents.

A girl of twenty-two left Texas, and tomorrow morning she will be a full-grown independent woman. I'm ready. I've got a lot to prove, especially to myself. And I'm here to learn how to play with the big guys in the big leagues.

I stuff the black leather briefcase with things like Post-its, pens and pencils, the works. I also go shopping to make sure I have the perfect attire. Apparently the CEO has a dress code.

My shopping is for uniforms, pieces in black, white, or gray, required for all Carma Inc. employees.

I come home to bags of popcorn accompanied by a note.

You can't call yourself a Chicago resident until you've tried this.
Your favorite bro.

I text him: **You're my only bro, meathead.**

T.R.: Only reason I'd be your favorite.

Me: Say hi to Gina. Turning in early. BIG DAY TO-MORROW!

T.R.: Babe, it's going to be a big day every day for 3 months. Carmichael is cool as a cucumber in everything except business. You've been warned.

Me: Challenge accepted.

T.R.: If you wimp out, you can intern with me.

Me: My favorite bro? So he'll give me time to file my nails and watch reality TV while at work? No thanks, I'd rather earn my place.

T.R.: K. Let me know when you miss being a princess and I'll see what I can do.

Me: Promise.

T.R.: Speak of the devil, got a dinner with your boss tonight.

Me: Please don't talk about me, I told you no special treatment because I'm your sister

T.R.: And I heard you the first time.

Me: Okay promise me!

T.R.: Sis, believe it or not we do have other things to talk about than you.

Me: Really? Then stop bugging me. I'm fine! I'm more than fine. Don't smother me, that's what Mom is for.

T.R.: I'd say we're done now.
Call me or Regina if you need anything.

Me: If I don't lose your numbers.

T.R.: HA.

I remember Gina has a key and she must've left the pop-corn there for me. I have the Garrett Mix popcorn for dinner and groan the whole time, even when I lick the remainder off my fingertips, then I wander into my bedroom, surprised to see a small basket of condoms on the bed.

Liv, don't tell Tahoe I left this, I just want to be sure you'll be smart about anything.
Love, Gina

I laugh and look at all the condom flavors in here, all of them in an extra-large size. I don't even wonder why Gina decided that is the most usual size because I'm pretty sure it's not, but okay. I hide the basket behind one of my picture frames on the lower shelf of the nightstand and then call my parents to finally tell them I'm settled in.

"All okay over there, Olivia? Did your brother help you settle in?"

"Mom. Any more and he and Gina will be moving in with me." I groan, but I laugh, too, so grateful to have a family that loves and supports me. I know nobody wants better for me than my family. I love my family, and I want them to be proud of me.

FIRST DAY

I wake up before the alarm clock, that's how nervous I am.

It's not only because I'll be facing my first official job, but because of *where*. I know the experience at Carma will give me an edge for when I go back to Radisson Investments and, later, create my own firm. Learning from the toughest raiding firm in the country will teach me the dirty games companies play—so I can learn how to stop them and protect the companies I hope to serve. But although I'm determined to learn as much as I can, I know that I need to make sure I walk away from Carma three months from now without losing my soul.

I don't want the experience to make me ruthless, like the rumors say about everyone who works at Carma.

I dress the part, though. Sharp corporate uniform: pencil skirt matched with a form-fitting cropped jacket. My hair back in a ponytail, low at my nape. It's elegant and it's sleek and I like how my hair feels close to my neck; it warms me. I'm very sensitive there. Any air at my nape tickles me. Next are pumps and pearl earrings. I want to accessorize, like using scarfs and bandanas on my ponytails and buns, but this isn't college. This is life now.

It's a hot, windy day in Chicago as I step out of the cab and look up at the building of Carma, Inc.

If the company's reputation isn't enough to intimidate you, the building should be.

Soaring high at over fifty-something floors, it not only seems to swallow me up as I stand on the sidewalk before its imposing glass doors, it also spreads out, side to side, to encompass the entire block.

Wow.

I can't believe this is where I will be working.

Today I'm to be briefed, along with a dozen other interns, on my duties.

I inhale, clutching my briefcase a little tighter to my chest.

Okay, then.

I lower my briefcase, and walk inside to my first official job.

Butterflies flap in my stomach as I ride the elevator to my floor. I see myself dressed in the required uniform. Goodness. I look scared. *Get a grip, Livvy!* I'm not sure if I will meet him today. Or ever. I don't want my brother's favor to extend to any special treatment and I made that clear, which means Tahoe probably made it clear to Callan Carmichael. I'm a working girl now.

Still I hope to do such a good job that he'll eventually hear about me. Oh yes, he'll be quite *happy* he brought me on!

All right, first day.

Thankfully, I will only have a first day here once.

Only a day in, and I've already heard about the newest takeover. It's talked about in the cafeteria and in every phone call my boss receives for the day. I've been assigned to the research department, working for Mr. Henry Lincoln. He is a kindly, historian-looking middle-aged man with a shiny bald head and a gruff voice, but warm eyes that always seem to stare off into space as if he's thinking of something else.

I'm assisting him in his research. He's one of Carmichael's most genius minds, and it is our job to find the businesses that require Carmichael's definite attention.

I'm not a girl who wants to specialize in takeovers, but to find companies that need help and find ways to acquire that help for them. But in order to do what I want to do in the future, I figured the best way to build a company up is to know how companies are usually taken down, and why. Reviewing each leg of a business and finding the weak spots is how sharks like Carmichael topple them and claim ownership. But finding the weak spot can also help me learn ways to rebuild and strengthen until—*voilà*—you have a healthy business again.

Part of the day I'm overwhelmed wondering if I'm cut out for this and desperate not to fail. Coffee, notes, folders, research.

Hostile takeovers are the name of the game. I need to research info on positioning—whether the business we're after is listed on the Dow or NASDAQ, investors, company history, capital investment, cash influx, costs of running, the works.

I have nine-to-five hours, but I linger today until 6 p.m., helping Mr. Lincoln finish the stacks of folders for the presentation with Carmichael and his board tomorrow.

I'm bringing the last set of copies from the copy room on the third floor along with Lincoln's fifth coffee when I set them on his desk—and spill his coffee right down my required gray jacket.

"Shit!" I mutter. "Mr. Lincoln . . ."

"It's fine. It's fine. We're nearly done here. Just go. Take that mess off. Just don't let anyone see you without it."

Feeling the coffee sticking against the fabric, I whip the jacket off.

"Go, I tell you," he says as he waves me off and keeps sorting the files.

I do go, but not before I refill his coffee and bring it back to his desk. "I'm sorry," I apologize.

"Stop apologizing—you're going above and beyond what any intern ever has on their first day. Go home and rest," he says again, kinder now that he sees I brought him coffee.

I nod and then head to the elevators, folding the jacket over my arm. Three elevators stop on my floor and each of them is bursting with people leaving. All of them staring at the stained jacket draped on my arm.

God!

Am I to go down as the intern who fucked up on her first day?

I click the up arrow and find the elevator heading to the top is absolutely empty.

I step inside and exhale, trying to regroup and waiting to leave until the entire building has left first.

I step onto a gorgeous terrace.

My breath catches when I spot something.

A dark figure at the far end, leaning on the railing.

He's wearing a white shirt and black slacks, the sleeves rolled up to the elbows. I can see the definition of his back muscles and the slim waist encircled by a sleek black belt, and the ass.

His backside is to me, and I blink because, what a fine backside it is.

A cigarette dangles from the corner of his mouth. I'm not a smoker, but suddenly I want to be.

He looks relaxed and on top of the world, and suddenly I want to be right on top of it and relaxed with him.

"Would it be terrible of me to ask for a hit?" I take a step forward.

He doesn't turn to look at me. He doesn't seem surprised I'm here. I suppose he heard the elevator ding when I stepped outside and he's used to others coming here.

He merely stretches his hand out, silent, and I see his forearm and the masculine veins there because maybe he works out.

I walk forward to where he leans over, looking at the city. "It's my first day here."

"Treat it just like any other day and you'll be fine."

I start at the deep voice. I take the cigarette from his fingers and take a hit, inhale, and I'm exhaling the smoke when I feel him look at me. I look back.

Lovely brown hair with light sun streaks throughout and a pair of eyes that are unsettlingly intense stare fixedly at me. They're fringed with dark, spiky lashes, and above them, a set of straight dark eyebrows. The rest of the features accompanying them start to filter into my brain, and I can't believe anything could be both this male and this perfect. Smooth fore-head, a nose that is elegant and a mouth that is strong, a jaw with perfect hard lines, a little scruff on it—but not a lot—and lips that make me, for some reason, very aware of my own lips.

I'm staring.

So stop staring.

"I . . . uh . . ."

They start to dance, those eyes.

"Do you want to light one?" His voice is more gravelly than before.

"What?"

He signals to the nearly extinguished cigarette, reaching into the inner pocket of his shirt to pull out a pack, and with a movement flicks open the top.

I'm thrilled to meet someone other than my brother and his girlfriend. This is one friend I'm making on my own.

I nod, afraid to reach out. He takes a cigarette between his lips, lights it, takes a drag, and hands it over to me, slowly blowing out a cloud of smoke that billows upward as he watches me, his eyes glimmering.

I take it, place it between my lips, and inhale. I exhale the smoke out slowly. "Thank you." I stay where I am. "I'm afraid of heights."

He turns and shifts his shoulder, eyeing me in curiosity now. "Any reason you're here, other than masochism?" His lips tilt a little.

So do mine. "My fear of heights keeps my other fears in perspective. When things start to seem crazy, I look for the highest place I can find and everything else feels manageable. It all feels smaller."

He gives me a smile that sends my pulse racing unexpectedly as he plucks the cigarette from my lips and buries it in the standing ashtray nearby as he says, "Come here, seriously, I won't let you fall."

I hesitate.

He tucks his cigarette pack into his slacks and easily, like it means nothing, reaches out to pull me a few feet closer to the edge. "See? Nothing to fear."

His pleasantly deep voice seems to sink into my stomach like an anchor, sending a little prick all over. I shiver. And then I realize this guy, this stranger, is touching me. His hand is on my waist, curving around me.

Um, hello, move, Livvy? I'm not the kind of girl who lets guys this close without a proper date.

I squirm a little. But his hands are *strong*. "You can let go of me."

"Can I really?" His eyes are still dancing.

"Yes, um. You can." I'm shaking. There's more amusement on his face.

He looks down at his hand, smiling, and raises his eyes with pure mischief. "Are you sure?" He scans me as if to make sure I've got my footing.

I nod. "I'm okay."

He lets go, looks at me with that same puzzled smile, then at his watch. "And I'm late."

I exhale and nod. "I'll just stay up here for a bit."

He pulls out his pack of cigarettes and sets it on the ledge, then winks at me, and walks away.

I stare at the cigarettes. I take one step, and another, and even if everything I ever wanted were waiting for me, sitting up on that ledge, I couldn't reach it if I wanted to.

HOT SMOKER GUY

I tell myself I'm not going upstairs today. But I find myself wandering up the elevators the next day, and up onto the terrace before I head home. It's not the terrace that has been niggling at my curiosity nonstop.

It's Hot Smoker Guy.

I'm not a girl who thinks a lot about guys. I hardly thought about them all through college, I was too busy trying to graduate. So this curiosity is a bit of a first, and maybe just a tad worrisome too.

He's wearing a blue polo today. It's kind of ballsy that he doesn't care about being fired because he's not wearing the requisite black-and-white or gray uniform everyone in the company wears. He is most definitely the mail guy.

"You don't care about the dress code either, huh?" I say.

He lifts a brow, apparently amused by the tone of approval in my voice.

"You're wearing a polo today, and the other time no jacket."

It seems impossible, but his eyes sparkle even more. "You know all about my dress habits?"

He seems amused and delighted by that, and for some reason, it makes me flush.

He turns the chair and sits before me, arms draped over the chair back. "What's the problem with the dress code? Looks to me you wear it very well."

I roll my eyes.

He's laughing at me.

"It's boring, that's what." I signal to him and his don't-give-a-shit attitude. "I just wish I had your balls."

"Where exactly do you want them?"

I laugh, then flush. Oh god.

He laughs too. "I'm sorry, that was completely out of line," he says shifting forward in the chair. "I couldn't resist."

"You know what? You really should," I say with a little frown. "Does anyone fall for those antics?"

"You'd be surprised how many women fall for my . . . antics."

I eye him dubiously. "If you say so." He has his charm and that face does him plenty of favors but the guy seems to have a gargantuan ego already, I'm not about to feed it any more. "And I meant the balls to not wear . . . the required clothing. How do you get away with it?"

"My special antics include charming my way past reception."

"It would help if the receptionists were male and maybe *I* could charm them."

He eyes me. "I'd bet on it."

"Seriously. It's one thing to be a perfectionist and another to be anal. Come on!" I sigh. "I don't want to disappoint my brother, though. He got me this job. But I intend to be the one to keep it."

He lifts his brows, scrutinizing me suddenly.

As if he just realized something life-altering.

I wonder if he has any ambitions other than being the mail guy. He's not putting out the vibes of someone desperate to climb the ladder of success.

I'm so busy wondering that I don't realize he's frowning thoughtfully as he stares down at his cigarette. He laughs softly, as if to himself, and then he rises from his chair, takes a step back and says, "Good night."

He grabs a jacket and his phone and keys, and walks out.

Did I say something wrong?

The next day, I spot him in the elevator.

The coworker who boards with us spots him too, and the instant she sees him, her spine shoots up straight. I'm surprised she's not fluffing her hair, though I don't blame her one bit. I suppress the urge to primp myself too. She nods politely at him as we ride to our floors. Hot Smoker Guy nods back, then looks at me. He doesn't nod. Just stares. I smile. We're left alone.

I'm impressed that my unambitious mail guy broke out the best suit he owns, dark black, and a tie that's just killer. Nobody would wear a red tie here unless they're interviewing, it would need to be silver or black.

"Look at you! Are you here for an interview?" I ask when we're alone. "You broke out your best suit."

He starts to laugh, then rubs his face with one hand and

shakes his head.

"We're matching." I point to the red scarf I'm wearing as a hair band, my one small rebellion against the dress code.

"Yeah, I'll have to do something about that," he says as he reaches out and tugs the scarf loose, tucking it into his pocket. Just like that. He crosses his arms in a nonchalant stance and stares at the climbing numbers.

He tilts his head to eye me, and I can't miss the way his gaze runs to my shoulders and to the fall of my hair. I become breathless.

I glance at my reflection in the elevator doors. Blonde and blue-eyed, fair-skinned, I look small and weak and he looks big and hot in that stupid suit.

"Will you be at the terrace this afternoon?" I blurt out.

His brows rise in surprise, and then his eyes run over my hair again, slowly and thoroughly.

It feels like forever before he speaks, his voice smooth and calm in a way that his stare is not. "I'll leave you my cigarettes, how's that?"

"Oh no, it's not the cigarettes. I don't even smoke, not really. I just . . . well, I don't have a lot of friends here, really. I like it when we share a cigarette on the terrace."

His eyes look a little tender, but that gorgeous mouth of his doesn't speak.

Thank god that finally my floor is up.

"Well, bye." I wave, smiling, and I step out awkwardly and force myself not to look back. *Shit. Fuck. Shitfuck!* I'm cursing to myself, feeling a flush creep up my cheeks, wondering why I care so much that he didn't say yes.

I still end up showing upstairs.

Still wondering why I even care. The last thing I want is a guy. In fact, I'm even wearing the small diamond ring my parents gave me on my fifteenth birthday on the fourth finger of my left hand, so the guys will leave me alone in case I ever go to a club or out with some of the other interns.

I suppose I just want a friend. And I like his energy. All easy confidence and male strength. It's something I adore about my brother. He makes me feel safe. But this guy is a stranger, so I don't understand, exactly, why I crave talking to him except that maybe I'm curious, and I feel a buzz of excitement when he's near.

He's standing by the ledge when I step out of the elevator. My heart leaps a little, and I have to take a deep breath in order to act cool when I join him.

He looks at me as if challenging me to walk close to the ledge.

I stop a few feet away and finger the hem of my black jacket. His eyes snag on the ring I'm wearing.

"Who's the guy?" he asks, casually, frowning down at the ring.

I laugh and glare at him. "Wow. What happened to your antics? Not 'who's the *lucky* guy'? I didn't miss the omission."

"I'm not sure if he's lucky, or terribly, terribly unlucky," he says.

I want to say a name out of the blue.

I sigh.

"It's a gift from my parents and the ultimate commitment to giving my goals my all."

"Really."

"Really."

He moves and I step back.

"So it's a phony."

"It's not a phony, it's a real diamond!"

"It's a phony engagement ring."

"It's not. I'm engaged to myself."

He shoves his hands into his pockets and rocks back on his heels. "Ahh, surely because nobody else would want you?" he asks, looking deathly somber.

I nod, also deathly somber. "Actually, that's precisely why. I've got clusters of freckles on every part of my body and a personality that's even worse."

"Worse than freckles." He scratches his chin.

"*Clusters* of freckles."

"You might find someone one day," he eyes the ring and then eyes me, "with a *freckle* fetish," he draws out, laughing. "And he'll see exactly why you're special. But that ring could deter him from even trying to discover all those *clusters of freckles* underneath."

I wonder what that would feel like. To be loved like that. In the way my brother loves Regina. My dad and mom love each other. "If he can't take a little competition and would let something like hardware prevent him from knowing me then I'm not interested. He gets none of my freckles."

He smiles quietly, and I wonder about him.

If he's ever loved, if he's ever been loved, if he even wants to be. But don't we all want to? Even when you think you don't want to, there's this feeling of waiting in the back of your head. Of waiting for that to happen. To know what it's like and to be swept away.

"I think I'll have a cigarette now," I say, flushing.

I can't believe I opened my big mouth, but I'm desperate for some real conversation and some silly conversation and to just be me, to talk with someone who won't judge me or look at me like the lowly little intern whose brother got her the job.

He lights up, and this time when I set the cigarette to my lips, there's a low throb deep in my stomach just knowing my lips are on the exact spot his were.

The wind tosses his lovely brown hair about recklessly. He gives the impression of control but in a way that makes you wonder what happens when all that power is unleashed.

"So. You have a brother," he says.

I nod. "Yep. He taught me to put my thumb on the hose and aim the stream at an angle to the sun so I could make a rainbow. We were silly like that. Though I hate his big-brother condescending bullshit. He wanted me to stay in his building in some posh apartment. I insisted I pay for an apartment I could afford with my salary."

He lifts his brows, impressed.

"He put money into a trust for me when I turned eighteen, but I haven't touched it. It's not mine. I want to know I can earn my keep . . . and then give it away to something special. Some noble cause." I shrug. "He makes plenty of donations, but I want to give something that comes from me so I can earn points up there." I point to the sky.

He listens attentively, the cigarette forgotten in his hand as he looks at me with the merest hint of a smile.

"I had a friend who died . . . of leukemia, so young. You only live once, and you never know how long you'll have to do anything, really."

"I'm all for going all in," he agrees.

"Me too. Or, I suppose I *was* all for going all in until a few failures made me a little less enthusiastic about it," I admit. "Like my first crush! So, my first crush was at camp, on a counselor. Mike Harris. He was older and of course so mature, and he swam like a shark. One day I decided to go for it and I kissed him, and he gently turned me down. Listing all the reasons why we shouldn't when all I wanted to know was if he wanted me back." I laugh. "We're still friends."

"Are you?"

"Why do you ask as if the concept is alien to you?" I burst out laughing. "Yes! We're friends. Guys and girls can be friends. I did camp every year, and he was there for several. I'm even friends with his wife, it was just a crush."

"Have you had many crushes?"

"A few." I laugh again. "But not another big enough to go after him like I did with Mike." I eye him. "You?" My voice goes soft, as if the mere word *you* is something intimate.

He takes a drag from his cigarette, frowning, as if trying to decipher the answer to my question. "I suppose I never let my infatuations run that long. When one starts, I nip it in the bud." He uses his free hand to make a scissor-like movement in the air.

"How so?"

"After a night or two."

"Just enough to get it out of your system? That's really dickish of you."

"*Dick* is the best word you have for me?" His laugh is low and deep and so very pleasant it makes me quiver.

"You seem to have a pretty big one on you—"

"I don't make any promises, though—"

We both speak at the same time and stop when we realize what I said.

My cheeks start to burn.

I can't stop thinking of his package now under his pants.

"Are you thinking about it now? It's liking the attention."

"Shut up!" I laugh and shake my head. "My mouth is always getting me into trouble. When I was a little girl and one of my mom's friends came to visit, I asked her flat out why she had the voice of a turkey. It wobbled!"

He reaches out as he simultaneously peers into my face, and when I realize he's going to brush my hair back so he can look at me as I tell my story, I nervously push it back and keep going.

"My mom couldn't apologize enough," I add.

Why did I do that? He was going to touch me and I stopped him.

I got too nervous about it . . . by the way he was looking at me.

I fall silent and drop my gaze to my feet, letting my hair fall back in a curtain as I hope recklessly that he'll try to do it again.

He doesn't.

"So why *did* she talk like a turkey?" he asks with a puzzled frown.

I laugh, and he laughs too.

It's weird. He makes me feel like he is so interested, like it's important for him to know.

"Are you this curious all the time?" I ask.

"Curious? I'm not curious, in fact I've zoned out this whole time." He makes a dismissive move with his head.

"*Zzzzz*, heard nothing."

I push at his chest, and he laughs and catches my wrist, and then my laughter traps in my throat and I can't breathe, because his touch zips down my body like a bolt of lightning.

"So, you wanted to know about my crushes," he says. "You were curious too. Do you have any lives left?"

"Only one, I think." I grimace and then grin.

"One's enough if you make the most of it, isn't it?" he asks softly, then passes me his cigarette, which is about done.

I thank him, but shake my head, declining, touched he was saving the last drag for me.

I want to ask him if he's doing anything this weekend. I want to see the sights, but I don't want to go alone and I don't want to be a constant burden to Tahoe and Gina, or the few interns I've met who seem about as lost as I am. But I don't. Instead I say, "Well, I guess I'd better get home."

It's only until I'm riding down the elevator that I realize I didn't ask him about his interview, or call him names because he stole my red hairband.

I suppose I wanted to have an excuse to talk to him again.

That weekend, Gina takes me out to lunch to meet her friends, Rachel and Wynn. They all ask about me, how I'm doing at Carma, and whether I've met Callan.

"No, but I'm happy I haven't. I warned Tahoe I wanted to do this on my own," I tell them.

"It's funny. Callan is such a good guy, but in business

he's very intense. He's like an apocalypse," Wynn says.

It makes me a little nervous just at the prospect of meeting him.

The conversation turns to them forcing me to eat a Chicago-style hot dog—no ketchup, they say. I chow down on one, the best hot dog I've ever had, and they insist I also must try a deep-dish pizza soon.

Gina confides in me she has a bet going on with my brother.

"Livvy, don't go to any clubs. I have a bet with him that if you go, as he suspects you will, he'll shave his beard. And I don't want him to shave it."

"I really don't care what my brother does with his beard, but I promise you if I go, he'll be the last to know."

That evening, when I get to my apartment, I get a call on my cell phone from Wynn—whose contact I just added while we were at lunch.

"It's Wynn, Livvy, I need to ask for a favor. About that club thing . . . the no-going-clubbing rule Tahoe set for you. Is that set in stone?"

I ask her why.

"My ex is at this club. I want to see him. I want him to see me looking amazing. And I want to see if we can talk, but I can't go alone, and Rachel and Gina would kill me. Please come, nobody will know. I'm renting nearby; you can sleep over at my place so you're not on your own late at night."

It's 9 p.m. and I'm already in my PJs, but I really liked Wynn, and I want to enjoy the city, so I tell her I'll be ready in twenty minutes.

I slip on a pair of tight jeans, a cropped sequined top, high heels, and pull my hair back in a ponytail. I add a red pearl necklace simply because I miss using color at work, and then Wynn texts me that she's in a cab downstairs, and I grab my keys, a small clutch purse, and head out, feeling a little guilty and sending a quick prayer for my brother to be blissfully ignorant about my escapade.

Thirty minutes later, I'm at a noisy club littered with booths, a huge dance floor, flashing lights, and music. Wynn is in a booth with a handsome blond guy, having a heated argument, and I'm people-watching when my eyes snag on a figure with lovely copper hair and a face to die for at the very end of the room.

Hot Smoker Guy?

When a couple of dancers obstruct my line of sight, I shift in my seat and stare disbelievingly. He's with another guy, deep in conversation, and I can hear his rumbling laugh through the music.

A girl sits on his lap, looking dotingly up at his face with eager puppy-dog eyes that beg for him to pet her.

He talks to his friend while the girl's fingers wander over his chest. Still, he ignores her.

I feel sorry for her, but it looks so comfortable on his lap that I'm sorry for me too.

I'm scowling when he absently scans the room and catches me staring.

His smile fades a bit as his gold eyes hold mine—and he gives me a look that rivals vaginal penetration. He uncurls his hand from the woman's waist and inches her off his thigh, leans forward, elbows on his knees, as if he wants to talk to me and only me.

I tilt my head up to hold his gaze, and the hunger/worry stomach pangs double in force. I give him a haughty look because I expect him to say something crass. He looks at my mouth, then lifts his drink and toasts.

He takes a sip, wetting his lips, and stretches his arm out over the woman again.

He smiles and watches me probingly. He seems to be waiting for me to walk up to him, but I'm trembling a little and I will die before he notices, so I stay in my seat.

I turn around and look at Wynn, and Hot Smoker Guy's gaze seems to follow.

Wynn seems to be trying to get to her feet, wiping tears from her eyes.

Hot Smoker Guy appears and helps her up by the elbow. He asks her something and nods.

Hot Smoker Guy looks up and sees me.

I smile at him, grateful for the help with Wynn, but he doesn't smile at me.

My stomach sinks and I look hastily away as he brings her over.

"I'll take her home." It's a statement, not a question.

"Wait. She's coming, too," Wynn protests.

There is a prickle of heat against my fingers; his hand engulfing mine totally. He's smirking, his gold eyes laughing as he scans me thoroughly, head to toe, and his lips—slightly warm in a way that makes my stomach lose control—brush against the shell of my ear, his voice all dark chocolate, wine, and foreplay as he says, "You really don't go here."

I scowl at him, then let him drag us both out of the club. We help Wynn into a cab, and he follows her in before tugging me inside, reaching over me to close the door.

My thigh brushes against his thigh. My throat feels tight.

"Just say the word and he'll be so swollen tomorrow he

won't be able to open his eyes." His words swallow the silence of the cab.

His voice, clear without the Chicago wind around us, pulses through my body. I stiffen to try to ignore its effect on me.

"Stop, no way. But thanks." She laughs mournfully.

He takes her hand and squeezes it and cups her face with the other. "Hey. You're good. You don't need some asshole who doesn't need you back."

She takes his hand and squeezes, says, "Thank you," and hugs him. He wraps one arm around her, and I want to vomit. I realize he's looking at me as he strokes his hand down her back, his stare so intense that it feels as if he's stroking his hand down *my* back.

I miss home so much right now I want to cry.

I don't know why I want to cry, but I edge my thigh away from his and move to stare out the window.

I hear him ask Wynn something about what happened, and Wynn tell him it's a long story, that they just won't work out.

He says he's sorry.

And he sounds genuinely sorry.

I feel like a third wheel all of a sudden, and I want to call my brother so I can have a guy's arms around me, telling me it'll just take one second, and it'll be over.

It takes a gazillion seconds before I leap out of the cab, avoiding his gaze even as he helps her out. I take one of her arms while he takes the other, and we head upstairs to the apartment and settle her on a living room sofa.

"Thanks," I say as I take off Wynn's shoes, and he looks at me with a frown.

"You okay?"

"Fine. Thank you. Now you know where she lives in case you want to . . . visit her when I'm not here or whatever . . ."

He lifts his brows, then I tell Wynn, "I'll get you coffee."

"You know where to find me," he tells Wynn.

"At the club?" I want to shout when the door closes behind him.

I exhale and inhale as I make coffee and try to push the odd homesickness away as I come back to Wynn.

"You okay?" I ask.

"Yeah. It was just difficult to talk to him. Emmett and I used to be so easy together, but now that he's my ex, it's like there's this whole wedge between us."

She seems better now. I take a couch opposite hers and curl my feet up under me. "How did you two meet?"

She sighs and stares into space. "He seduced me with food and that smile he has."

"I'm sorry, Wynn. Should I call Gina or Rachel?"

"Don't even think about it! They'll kill me, and they'll absolutely kill *you* for being there." She looks at me and her expression softens. "Thank you, Livvy. I promise nobody will know."

I won't ask, I won't ask, I won't ask, I repeat like the mantra. Then I ask. "Hey, the guy who brought you home—"

She waves a hand. "Oh, I totally warned him not to say a word."

I bite down on my lower lip, still aching to know. "Who is he?"

She quirks an eyebrow at the anxiousness in my voice, and her big blue eyes widen even more.

"He works where I work, so . . ." I hasten to explain.

"Hell, I *know*." She eyes me in amusement, then scowls in puzzlement. "Ask him."

Now I'm thinking: *I am not going to ask her, it's really not my business.* And then, "Did he and you . . ."

"What? Ohmigod, never! He's a one-way ticket to Broken Heartsville, even worse than Emmett."

So they're just friends? *Thank you, god.* Though I thought he and I were friends too but he doesn't cozy up to me in that way. He tried to touch my hair and I moved it back before he could and that was the extent of it.

"He's single, if that's what you want to know," Wynn says. Then her eyes go a little wider in concern as she says, like this is crucial for me to know, "He's like the testament to singleness. All his friends are taken, so now he's the last man standing. Please don't tell me you like him. He's the last man Tahoe would like to see you with. Trust me."

"I don't like him. Not at all. I'm not . . . interested in anything like that. This is why I have this fake engagement ring, see?" I show her my hand. "This'll keep all the guys away, even at clubs. This year is all about work for me. I want to go back to Texas and get some more experience, then open my own investment firm, helping struggling businesses."

"Good for you." She looks wistfully past her shoulder, out to the window. "Love is an illusion. The more you want it, the more it hides."

"You'll get back together with him. Your ex, I mean. I saw the way he looked at you. When you stood up crying, he wanted to come after you but held himself back."

"Emmett?" She turns her attention back to me, looking sad again. "I don't think so. He flat out said he didn't want marriage. I thought after I moved in, it would be in the cards.

We just don't want the same things." She sounds wistful, and then she frowns and waves it away. "Anyway. Guard your heart, Livvy, you're too young, and I've seen too many men steal hearts without giving anything back."

I should have listened.

But the next day when I'm done with Mr. Lincoln and the preparations for his presentation with Callan Carmichael, which will take place the following day, I feel compelled to ride the elevator up to the terrace again. I tell myself I'll just thank him for looking out for Wynn. It was gentlemanly, I suppose.

Though maybe his reasons for helping her were just to seduce her because, apparently, he's an expert at that.

He's not there.

I ride up to the terrace on Tuesday, then on Wednesday.

He isn't there.

It isn't until Friday that I step out of the elevator, already expecting him not to be there, when I see him seated in a lounge chair at the far end, a cigarette dangling from his lips as he types something on his phone, frowning in concentration.

I don't want to feel the rush of happiness. But I do. It comes with a tangle of pain in my stomach, and that I cannot explain, but I blame it on the terrace railing and the fact that I'm . . . well, not happy at high altitudes.

Funny how the tangle wasn't here when *he* wasn't here, though.

I approach and sit down next to him, and he doesn't look up from his phone. Once he types something, he puts out his cigarette and looks at me with a smile.

The tangle loosens as if someone burnt the ends and it exploded in a ball of warmth.

"Where were you?" I ask.

"Around," he says.

I'm feeling bold and admit, "Well, I missed sharing a cig with you."

I grin mischievously, but his answering grin is about a thousand times more mischievous than mine.

"I couldn't resist not seeing you either," he says, low.

Nervous by his nearness and realizing how much he seems to mean it, I reach out for the cigarette pack and the lighter sitting to his right, and he covers it with one big hand. "These trips to the terrace are terribly bad for you," he warns, still smiling with those hazel eyes.

"Cigs are as bad for me as they are for *you*."

He's silent for a moment, making me wonder if he was even referring to smoking. Then he *tsk*s softly, as if I'm a naughty girl but he seems to kind of like it, and then he lights one up. I watch him, a little breathless as he cups the flame then hands it over. I set my lips around it and they tingle because he just had his mouth on it. I can taste him on the cigarette. I can taste him in the air.

I don't want to do either but I can't seem to force myself to stay away. He's like the highlight of my day.

I inhale, then exhale the smoke and put out the cigarette on the clear ashtray on the coffee table before me instead of passing it over to him, suddenly feeling too intimate to share a cigarette.

"Does this brother of yours know you were out club-bing?" he then asks, looking at the cigarette I just extinguished as if wondering why I didn't want to share today. He's sitting with his elbows on his knees, looking sideways at me, his stare once again playing havoc with me.

I shrug. "Why?"

He leans back and links his fingers behind his head, watching me with a growing frown as he studies me even more, as if I'm this complicated thing. "I wouldn't want my little sister in those kinds of clubs."

"You have a little sister?" My voice reveals my utter sur-prise.

"No," he says slowly, eyes twinkling.

"Fine so tell me where a girl's supposed to go. Or better yet, take me there."

His eyes widen in surprise, but then his lips twitch, and his eyebrows slowly start rising. "The places I frequent aren't exactly ones a girl with . . . *clusters* of freckles belongs in." He smirks.

I start to blush. I can't help it. I can't help wanting to know more about him.

I want to do more than that; I want to kiss him.

I've never wanted to kiss this way before. With my whole body, hands and legs and tongue.

"I wanted to go see the sights this weekend. I haven't seen anything but my apartment and Carma since I got here, and I've heard there's so much to see," I say, searching that gorgeous face for an inkling of whether he'd like to come. "But tonight I just wanted to go to a bar and have a drink or two."

"That bad a day, huh." He studies me in understanding,

and it only makes me want to kiss him more.

"Worse," I say, nodding in exaggerated dismay.

He passes me my jacket. "Put on your jacket, then. Let's get some drinks."

"I've planned on working for a company from twenty-two to twenty-five, then start my own business by twenty-six, and maybe at twenty-eight, I'll meet my husband."

"Really?"

"Well, he won't *know* he's my husband but . . ."

"What's he like?"

"Hmm. He's kind and giving, and he . . . well, I suppose I never feel like I say or do the wrong thing with him."

He eyes me in amusement and links his fingers behind his head. "Why twenty-eight?"

We're at this cute little bar a few blocks from Carma. We sit side by side at the counter. I'm on my third glass of white wine, and he's drinking red.

"Seems like a good number."

"I'm twenty-eight. Does this mean I need to keep an eye out for my wife?" He snickers the word.

"In *my* plan it does." I laugh. "What's your age?" I frown. "To meet the one."

He grimaces.

"Really," I press.

"I haven't the mind for that."

"Why?"

Silence.

"You don't want kids?" I ask.

"I like kids, but I'm not sure I can be responsible for one."

"Well, that's where the wife comes in. You might want one if you're going to have kids."

"Haha."

His smile relaxes then morphs into that boyish face of his for a moment. Until it's suddenly gone. "I don't know that I can love someone that deeply," he says. He frowns as if remembering something, and he glances at his glass and strokes his thumb around the rim. "I'm not built that way."

"Fine keep your bimbos. I don't care."

"I will."

He laughs, his eyes lighting up again for the merest second before . . . they don't. His brows draw together in an agonized expression. "I'll just let her down," he says, gritting his teeth and glaring down at his wineglass. "I'm never falling into that trap."

"It's not a trap."

He shoots me a don't-be-naïve look. "Trust me. It's a trap."

"You just want crazy sex, then."

"Oh, I've had crazy sex. I'm good at that."

"You like it better than normal sex?"

"Depends on who you're doing it with. Crazy sex fills in for other things that I'm not exactly interested in just now."

"I've only had sex three times. Though the first one absolutely doesn't count, it was so awkward! He was grunting and done and I was left wondering, is this it?"

He peers into my face and lifts his hand as if to push my

hair back, but I quickly do it myself and nervously—because I'm suddenly mortified I admitted it to him, but why am I unable to stop?—add, "I consulted with my friends and they said it so wasn't it, so a few months later I went at it with a different guy. It was better, a little nicer. Not addictive though."

He brushes the other side of my hair, the one I didn't push back, and the touch frissons down my body like a lightning bolt. "And the third?" he asks gently.

"I don't know." I shrug, swallowing as I watch him shift in his seat to face me and cross his arms as if to keep them to himself. "It wasn't awkward, but it was still missing something. I've always thought sex is the moment you know when, well, you've found someone. It's always felt like that's missing so far."

"According to your plan you still have six more years to get to the meaningful sex. With your ignorant husband."

"Ignorant? He's not ignorant."

"He's ignorant of the fact that he's going to be your husband."

"Well, yes. For now." I grin.

"So how do you like working at Carma?" He drains the last of his wine.

"Oh, I don't work there. I just use the terrace." I sip on mine.

"In a uniform?" He asks for a refill on his.

"Well, if I don't wear it, I'd never get through security. The uniforms make me inconspicuous. Who knew what a black skirt and jacket could do?"

He watches me, and I lift my wine and drink. He loosens the top two buttons of his shirt and rolls his shirtsleeves to his elbows.

His sort of lazy, relaxed look makes my nipples bead.

I'm not sure if he's equally affected by my nearness as I am by his, but I'm crackling like live wires under my skin.

When I hear a song I like start playing, "TiO" by Zayn, I head to the small free space where a couple is slow dancing and I start dancing on my own.

He leans back, and he looks so delicious, so calm and powerful, I'm weak.

His hair is a little disheveled and the shadow on his jaw a little darker as he sits with his back to the bar, facing me. He pulls out a cigarette. Watching me very predatorily and scanning the room to see who else is watching me.

I don't think it's legal for him to smoke in here—but he doesn't seem bothered by that at *all*.

He lights up.

He wants me, I know that now, and as I smile at him and swirl my hips and move to the music, all I want him to see is the woman he wants *tonight*.

I love the playful sensuality in his eyes—like he's relaxed and nothing else exists but the drink in his hand, this bar . . . and me. Definitely me. Dancing and looking at him. Because there, right under the playful sensuality, is a heat I've never seen before.

A heat that makes me hotter than the sun.

He takes a drag, the tip glowing bright pink as I head back to the bar. When I reach him, he offers it to me. I can't take it, it feels too intimate now. I shake my head, and he only studies me as I drop to my seat, a little breathless.

He turns his high-backed stool a bit to face me, a silence between us as he smokes his cigarette and seems to take in my features, one by one.

I watch him take a hit.

"I think about kissing you," I hear myself say.

He exhales the smoke through a line between his lips and pushes the cigarette down on the ashtray and peers into my face, moving the curtain of my hair aside. "How do you kiss me?" he asks.

"I put my hands in your hair and . . . go up on my tiptoes and press my mouth against yours."

"No tongue?"

"I . . ."

I raise my head.

I'm used to guys looking at me. They stare when I walk down the sidewalk, when I'm on the dance floor, when I'm at Starbucks. I suppose I'm pretty, though I've always tried to downplay it by wearing minimal makeup and simple hairstyles like a bun, my hair loose, or a ponytail or a braid. I haven't gotten my hair professionally styled my whole life. I have good, manageable hair. Long legs, a slim form, perky breasts and an ass that's where it's supposed to be, thanks to yoga and running and squats. I'm natural, and I like it like that. But compared to the women I saw with him at the club, I feel plain and uninteresting.

And yet I know that, as plain and different as I am from those women, my Hot Smoker Guy wants me.

He has a *hard-on.*

He wants me, and he has no idea what I'm about to do.

Oblivious to the fact that I plan to strip him to his bones tonight, he smiles when the bartender asks if we'd like another and sips the last of his wine, chatting with him for a second, then sliding a credit card over the counter, facedown.

"Think I should take you home," he says.

His eyes meet mine. He's the hottest man I've ever seen. Down to earth and very centered for a mail guy. I think of the basket of condoms at my place. And especially of the tingle between my thighs. I've never felt it like this before. I need to suppress the urge to squirm under his appreciative hazel eyes, really.

"That would be nice." I walk without glancing back, my heartbeat pounding faster and harder as I step outside. I'm trembling, but I don't want to spend another night wanting and waiting. I mean to take what I want from him.

"We can just take a cab," I say.

He clicks something on his phone and says, "I got it."

"Uber? Oh."

A car arrives almost instantly, and I climb in the back. My heart is galloping in my chest all the way to my apartment building. I have never done something like what I'm about to do. I want to feel the freedom of making my own choices, of being grown up, *feeling* grown up, doing something that I want —really, *really* want—without worrying about the conse- quences.

"Would you walk me up?" I clutch his fingers and look at him.

He follows me into the building and up the elevator, my pulse fluttering madly at his nearness. I open my apartment door and bravely reach out to pull his hand and tug him inside.

I let go when he steps inside and shuts the door, and I turn to find his eyes on me, gleaming in the shadows.

I step forward and press my breasts against his chest. He grabs my hips and pins me in place with his firm grip, studying me with hot eyes. "What are you doing?" He drags the back of a finger down my cheek. "For someone afraid of heights, you like living on the edge." He grabs my hair and pulls my head back, his eyes fierce.

I slip my fingers into his hair. "Don't you want this?"

He lowers his head, and I go up on my toes and raise myself to meet his kiss. His lips capture mine, our tongues moving slowly to meet. It's like two lightning bolts crashing. His tongue flicks inside, and the touch sends shivers of desire through me.

We start to kiss more deeply, more wildly.

God. I'm being kissed from the inside out. His hunger only feeds mine.

His mouth, his hands, the heat of him, the scent of him, the feel of him, the taste of him. Sensation stimulation overload, and the slow buzz of the wine turns into a full-on high from a drug called Hot Smoker Guy.

No guy has ever kissed me like this, or made me feel this way.

He tears his mouth free and a gasp of protest leaves me.

His breathing is heavy, his pupils deliciously dilated.

"If I had any decency at all, I'd leave right now."

I shake my head. "Because we work together? We're not even in the same department." I rub my hands over his chest and his whole body tightens. "I want to be a woman. I want to be the woman that the man I want wants back. Don't you want me?"

"You know the answer to that," he says in a gravelly voice.

He's hard as steel against his slacks and my mouth waters. Emboldened by the feel of his erection against my stomach, I go up and start raining kisses on his jaw. "Then please. Look, I don't know the first thing about you, but I feel like I know you. Are you married?"

"God, no, I thought we cleared that up."

"I'm not either. You're not gay, judging by . . ."

"What department are you in?"

"What does it matter? Are you pulling a Mike Harris on me? Please don't pull a Mike Harris on me."

His eyes shine tenderly on my face, and he slides his fingers around my nape and holds my hair.

My throat closes as I look into his eyes. "I've always believed you regret the things you don't do more than the things you do."

"I'm actually a member of that same club." But he still seems hesitant, a battle in his eyes.

"Well, see! And we're both single, we're both consenting adults . . ."

He presses his thumb to my lips to quiet me.

My breath catches when the look in his eyes registers.

He places his fingers on my cheek and rubs them sinuously down my face. My breathing becomes erratic as he slides lower. I hear the rustle of fabric as he caresses his hand down the side of my clothes.

My hand steals into his hair and I set my lips on his ultra-sexy mouth, softly, and the second my lips touch his, I realize that he was waiting for my lips, for my kiss again. The moment our lips touch, he immediately turns what was my kiss into *his* kiss. Again.

He pulls my leg up by the knee and nestles his erection against me.

I press closer. "Oh god."

He holds my face in one hand. He opens my lips wide and his tongue flashes, irreverent and unapologetic and tasting of wine, into my mouth. "You taste so sweet." He tastes me deeper, as if he wants more, and holds me even closer. "You're so sweet," he says in an even huskier voice, his every thrust stoking the fire burning between my legs, every flick of his tongue hardening my nipples.

His kiss is warm, wet. He pops open the top button of my shirt and turns his head, lowers it and kisses the upper swell of one of my breasts, squished against him. He licks it and groans and squeezes me tight.

We embrace as we kiss, his hands on my back now, his fingers spread. I feel everything, front to front, his frame swallowing mine in a cocoon of muscles, strength and warmth.

He edges back in the darkness, and pulls me down on the couch and draws me over his lap to straddle him.

It's dark. The only sounds that of wet kissing and whispers. Raw and hoarse. I'm straddling him, his hands jammed beneath my skirt and under my panties. One hand cupping my butt, his thumb caressing the fissure.

Breathing and panting as we keep kissing.

"This okay …" he asks me. "How drunk are you?"

"I'm not drunk. Just buzzed." I cup his jaw and rock against him. "You?"

"I'm wasted." He runs his hand over my butt. "I'm so wasted." He licks my lips.

We're kissing again.

I stop, gasping. Our eyes meet and there's a question in his. His pupils are dilated, his eyelids heavy. "I don't remember if I shaved my legs this morning. I've been so focused on work—" I begin.

"I don't care." He runs his hands over my curves.

"Can I … can I just go get my razor very quick?"

He nods.

"Do you want me to shave down there?"

"Excuse me?"

"My friends say some guys prefer . . ."

"No. I want you as you are."

"Every cluster of freckles too?"

"I want those most of all."

He's pacing when I come out.

Our eyes meet and hold. He starts crossing the distance between us and I start walking and we meet halfway. He lifts me up by the ass and takes my mouth with his. His fingers bite into my ass cheeks and grind me to his erection.

"Do you have condoms?" I ask. "I've got—"

"I got it." He crushes my mouth again and three seconds later, I'm on my bed and he's on top of me, his lips tasting the skin on my neck.

He strokes his hand down the center of my chest. "Close your eyes and let me in."

I close my eyes and arch up.

He kisses my ear, his breath hot. Haggard. "Say you can handle what I'm about to do to you." His hand strokes a line down my torso, between my breasts, over my belly button. "Once I'm in, I'm owning every freckle I find. Just don't let me in here." He brushes his hand over my breast, over my heart.

I arch as his touch trails beneath my belly button.

"Do you like what you feel?" he asks.

I can't talk. He's cupping my sex beneath my skirt, the only thing separating me from him are my panties.

"Open your eyes."

I do.

"Do you like what you see?" he asks.

I swallow and touch his face. "Is this really happening?"

His lips curl a little. "That I'm going to sweep your hair off your shoulder and sweep you off your feet?" He pushes my hair off my shoulder and kisses me there.

I shiver.

He moves his hand to lift my skirt slowly up my thighs. "I'm about to turn up the heat now."

I can't breathe. "I'm scared."

"Don't be scared."

I grab his face between both my hands and bob my head up and down frantically, scared beyond reason. "I want you so much."

"I want you too." He lifts me up by the arms so that the back of my head rests on my pillow, and he licks at my neck, nibbling gently. "Touch me," he says.

I run my hands over his chest. He unzips my skirt and yanks it down my legs, and my panties follow. "Do you want me here?" He touches my wet folds and inserts one finger inside me.

Again, my head bobs frantically up and down.

He smiles slowly.

"And here." He rubs my clit with his thumb and moves his middle finger inside me.

I grab his shoulders and bite a piece of his shirt, gasping against the cotton.

"You're very beautiful. I hope every man who's ever been where I am now has told you," he rasps.

Um, no . . .

He bites on my neck a little, and then on my stomach, dips his tongue into my belly button until I'm about to come, then drags his mouth back up to lave and suck my nipples. "And these are the prettiest little freckles I've ever seen."

I flush. I can't imagine how many "freckles" he's seen.

"Roll over."

"I . . ." I'm trembling, but I obey. My emotions skid and whirl.

I feel his hands trailing down my back, as if he wants to find every flaw and spot and mark on my body. I feel him lean over and start to nibble on my ass, and he steals a hand between my cheeks to stroke my folds again.

I fist the sheets at my sides. My eyes are blurry, my breath is too fast to even really oxygenate me, I can't hear well because of the pounding of my heart and I can't smell anything past him. My senses have been reduced to feeling and to *him*.

Suddenly, he rolls over to his back, sits up and yanks off his shirt, pulls off his slacks, and lies back down—fully naked and holy . . .

God.

HOLY GOD.

I'm gaping at his cut body, his tanned skin, his huge . . . Oh god.

His lips curve as he says, "Come get it."

One breath,

Two breaths,

Three breaths,

And my lungs still feel empty of air.

He's got the biggest, hardest, longest, thickest erection I've ever seen.

He clenches his jaw and sweeps my hair aside, watching me. His eyes glow like fire in the night and he slides his hand around my waist and slowly drags me to his lap.

"Take me in," he urges.

He catches me by the ass and lifts me, my legs straddling him as our lips smash and he lowers me over him.

I gasp when he fills me.

I adjust over him.

My eyes hold his, cling to his, widening as I take him inside me—long, hard, pulsing with life. He won't take his eyes off me. They're heavy and male, and looking at me as if I'm some living masterpiece. There's not enough air in the world to fill my lungs right now. He's breathing just as hard, trailing his hands up to caress my breasts.

I moan softly and stay still over him.

He groans and sits up, grabbing my hair and rocking his hips beneath me. I wrap my arms around his neck and start rocking faster.

His hands span my waist firmly and he starts to get control of the rhythm even though I'm on top. He's setting the pace with every thrust, guiding me up and down.

We're watching each other.

He rocks his hips and I feel him—so hard, so big, so close —and I get wetter and wetter, absorbing everything.

The soft sucking motions of his mouth on my nipples arrow down to my sex, which keeps squeezing around him.

God, he's a sucking machine.

I run my fingers up his chest and let my mouth wander, tasting his jaw and his ear as he starts biting gently into my neck, his voice gruff as he tells me I'm so hot, so wet, so good. He's warm, sweaty, and salty.

He lifts me with one arm and then thrusts me down, pulling my head back, watching my neck arc, and he tells me, "Let's see what other freckles I find."

He bites my neck and nibbles, and I groan.

We lose control, stop talking, biting, licking, moving, groaning and fucking. Then my muscles are locking up and I'm racing for it, needing it. Needing *him*. I'm twisting and thrashing as I come, gasping from the intensity.

He tenses with a soft laugh-groan. He groans a pleasure sound that makes me come even harder and pushes me down on his cock as he jerks inside me. He growls something that sounds like *you feel so good* and rolls me over and finishes with a few greedy thrusts that somehow retrigger my orgasm.

My orgasm is like I've nothing experienced before. A detonation that shatters me to a billion nano-pieces.

When we're done, he cleans up as if we hadn't just had a mind-blowing sex session.

I lie comatose in bed. I'm on a high that has nothing to do with the alcohol. I'm catching my breath, sweaty and aware that my muscles feel completely weightless, while I watch him search his clothes. He lifts his cigarette pack and I grin, forget about my buttery muscles and go open a window. We lie on the bed, smiling at each other as we light up.

I start wondering his name as we alternate drags. Maybe Drake.

"Drake. That's your name."

"If I'm Drake, you're Mindy."

"No way."

"No way I'm Drake, Fanny."

"Hmm . . . Donathon?"

We start thinking up ridiculous names for each other until I say, "Good night, Harietto."

"Good night, Pippa." He strokes a hand down my back and whispers in my ear, "I enjoyed doing a thorough search for those *clusters* of freckles."

I wake up in darkness. Red neon lights a few feet away blink as the number strikes 3:28 a.m.

I'm curled against him. The memory of what we did rains down on me, soft as rose petals. I press my eyes shut, shifting closer and peering into his face. We had the hottest sex of my life, and I still want more. I want him inside me.

I'd never had an orgasm with a guy before, only on my own.

My world still feels a little off its axis.

His eyes are closed, his chest rising evenly. I'm in his arms, well, one of them at least. And it feels so nice! I could keep him as a muscular teddy bear. And a wicked sucking machine. And a free smoke, and well, I really *do* feel a little bit taken with him. Not that he's in my plans. But here I am. I have never before felt more like a woman, and he's holding me like he very much wants this particular woman to not get away. His arm is almost like a vise—but even that feels . . . so, so nice!

I touch his lips and settle deeper into his arm around me, craving the closeness. Craving all this nice.

I wake again to a ringing phone that doesn't sound familiar.

I stir and see a very gorgeous, disheveled man getting out of the bed, gifting me a glimpse of his ass. Sunlight streams through the window and he looks so perfect, I can't even think.

He slips into his slacks and pulls out his phone. "What time is it?" I ask groggily, sitting up in bed.

He checks his watch and zips up. "Eight. I've got to go." He raises his ringing phone, then takes the chair at the corner of my room and strokes the top of his head as he answers with a crisp, "Yeah."

My temples are throbbing from last night's wine. But my brain is whirling because of *all* of last night. My hair is tangled and I run my fingers through it as I sit on the bed, watching him. He smiles mischievously at me as he listens to someone on the other end of the line.

I get the tingle. Suddenly just thinking about that sucking thing he does. Just looking at him and that chest. He has a swimmer's body, lean and muscular but not overly so, and I find that very hot. As you can tell by the rampant hormone-fest of last night. I drop the sheet to my waist to see if I can entice him to come back to bed when he finishes his call. The idea of spending all Saturday morning with my sucking machine makes me sweat a little bit.

I drop the sheet farther down and watch his eyes start to blaze as they trail over me.

"Your sister? No, I've got other things on my mind. I just closed a deal that took months. I'll check in with her this week. Get an update from Lincoln."

His eyes suddenly watch me as he listens, and I see him spot a picture on my nightstand of my family and the realization seems to hit him the same instant that it hits ME.

He said "sister" and "Lincoln," and the panic is suddenly so overwhelming I can't breathe.

He looks at me, and I suddenly can't move.

"T, something's up." He hangs up.

We're both quiet.

He looks at me, all naked in my bed. All naked and thoroughly *fucked* by him. In my bed.

"Olivia," he says, softly.

I swallow. "Callan."

He drags his hand over his face.

His mouth is all red and kissed by me. *Oh. My. God.*

"I'm very, very late," he says.

"Yes. Go. Please."

So I slept with my boss. My boss's boss. Also my brother's friend. The guy who'd always been *off-limits*. The womanizer, everybody claims.

I feel like puking. I almost wish I could puke already, so I can get rid of the nausea.

The lines of concentration deepen around his eyes and mouth, and a shadow of disappointment crosses his face as he glances at the door. "I'd better go."

"Yes. Go."

I pull the sheet up and I want to hide from him, everything that yesterday I was too eager to show him. There's a silence as he opens the door, a hesitation, then I hear him shut the door.

I don't think I move from where I sit in shock on the bed for the next hour.

NOT THE MAIL GUY

I refuse to think of him sucking my breasts. Filling me up. Calling me beautiful. Talking to me, listening to me. Oh god.

I take a bath and stew and feel like I swallowed a bowling ball all morning.

You could say I feel a little bit uncomfortable now that I had sex with the boss.

The boss's boss.

Big whopping *whoops!*

Shit, really. Mega shit. I want to hide—better yet, die!

Well. *That's* not happening again.

Sometimes you think you have it all figured out. Get hooked on a detail. Make an assumption and that is the law in your eyes. An assumption that won't let you see anything else even when it's staring you in the face in a red tie. And once you finally see the big picture you feel so stupid to not have known. To have written down some theory as law. You feel so stupid. I feel so stupid I have replayed every scene in my mind, focusing on all the ways I should've been alerted that he was Callan Carmichael.

The women at the club.

The nervousness in the elevator when he boards.

Him wearing whatever he wants, he's the boss not the mailman! He's like a hero and a god at Carma and we are the worshipers.

I was too blind because I liked the idea of him being a mailman or some outside consultant or something.

I preferred thinking he was just a sexy mailman because that is something I could have.

The CEO, best friend to my brother, and my boss's boss, nope, wildly not happening and it's a little sad because I just had the best sex, the best night, of my life with him. From the moment I met him, I've wondered about him endlessly—hell, I've almost taken up smoking just to have an excuse to talk to him! And now. God.

Okay, so the man delivers—but *not* the mail.

It's been two hours since he left and I've changed my sheets and made my bed and am still smelling his cologne in my nostrils. Now I'm staring at my laptop but all I can think of is how the hell I'm going to bear going back to work on Monday. My brain cannot wrap itself around the fact that all this time I've already met the notorious Callan Carmichael. I've been spilling my guts out to him.

We fucked.

Well and good.

I groan, hating how much I want him to go back to being just Hot Smoker Guy.

He made me come so hard my body is still tingling, and then in the middle of the night, we had sleepy sex, and he made me come again, just as hard or even more because I was all dazed and relaxed and over-sensitized already.

Pushing him out of my mind, I grit my teeth and start reading all the investment sites, reminding myself of the reason I'm in Chicago.

I spend all morning studying companies and trying to come up with a proposal of my own to show Mr. Lincoln.

It feels like I was driving 100 miles per hour on the career front, very determined, but now, *now* it's like I'm ready to go at 1,000 miles per hour, full speed ahead. The takeover king took me over last night and I am ready to show him that sex is not all I'm good at. If he even liked it like I did.

Well shit, now I wonder if he did!

Forget about it. Focus on the plan. Learn from the master. Work the next few years. Save companies: win/win.

So I work for hours nonstop, all while Bloomberg plays on TV.

I take a break to halfheartedly munch on a sandwich and stare out the window at the sunny skies. But all I'm seeing is the saliva gland-stimulating sight of Callan lying in my bed, taunting me to *come get it.*

Suddenly I need to get out of this apartment before I lose my mind.

I change into jeans and a long-sleeved top and am wondering where to go when I get a text from Tahoe.

What are you up to?

I'm planning to go sightseeing in a bit

With?

Me.

Where you off to?

Maybe Art Institute?

I'll meet you there.

Really?

Really. I want to talk.

I don't know what he wants to talk about but my stomach won't stop twisting when I arrive at the Art Institute of Chicago to find my brother leaning by the entrance. He asks me what I want to see and we head in the direction of The New Contemporary exhibit.

I've enjoyed contemporary art ever since the time he invited me to New York, where he bid on a huge collection for his new apartment. He bought mostly Impressionist works and the best Van Gogh on the block, but we lingered in Manhattan for a few days, and I ended up falling in love with the contemporary art auction most of all.

I love new artists, so bold, trekking where no one has trekked before. I wonder when we look back on our generation, what we will see. Not just technology.

We head into the spacious gallery. It's peppered with masterpieces spaced strategically apart, giving the viewers the perfect space to contemplate one artwork at a time. "How's work?" he asks me.

I avoid making eye contact. "Good."

"You're with Henry Lincoln, right?"

I stare at a painting. I *refuse* to think of *him*, our talks and our cigarettes and our night of mind-blowing sex.

"Carmichael told me he'd check in on you this week."

I scowl. "I don't want him to, remember? I don't want special treatment." *Especially when I already got some.* Oh god.

I stare at a Warhol work—a self-portrait.

We start discussing some of the pieces as we go along, but I only seem to be agreeing and I'm frustrated that I don't even seem to have any personal input to offer.

"Livvy," he finally says, drawing me over to a nearby bench.

"Yeah?"

I can't breathe. Guilt does that. Everything seems to be about "it," that thing you did that you never, ever should have.

"I'm proposing to Regina."

It takes me a moment to register his words, and then they hit me like a truck at full speed. "What? Tahoe!"

"Keep it down." He's grinning ear to ear—the fool—as he draws me back to my feet and into the next gallery. And when I cannot talk, when I cannot say a thing, he says, "You're going to cry, aren't you?"

"No."

"You sound like it."

"Well I'm not. It's such a big deal! Shit. Well. Maybe I *am* going to cry, but I'm not going to do it here. God—is that the ring?"

He opens a velvet pouch and lets the ring slip into my palm. I just blink. He lifts it and shows it to me up close. A huge, brilliant round diamond set in a sleek platinum Tiffany band, *mesmerizing*, classic and timeless, the quality better than I've ever seen in my life.

"You picked it yourself?"

"That's right."

And it is so hard not to cry right now.

I fluff my brother's hair, then hug his big body against mine. "I love you, Tahoe," I say a little emotionally. I kiss his jaw and his beard pricks my lips.

"Love you too." He rumples my hair and stores the ring back in the pouch and shoves it into his jeans pocket.

I get the phone call from Gina later that night. She tells me the news and that their friends are throwing them an engagement party and Tahoe and she would like to pick me up on their way there.

I don't usually dawdle on my looks that much, usually I'm easy about it, but being in a corporate suit all week really makes it enjoyable to have an excuse to pull out a cute white lace skirt and a gold shimmery satin spaghetti-strap top. I'm also nervous because I'm afraid I'll see him there, and I need to look *good* to cover the fact that I feel utterly stupid.

I wear my hair loose, add a dab of lipstick, and slip my feet into my four-inch gold heels, then I head downstairs.

I climb into the back of my brother's Ghost, and from the backseat, I reach out and hug Gina and tell her, "I always wanted a sis!"

She squeezes me back meaningfully and I grab my brother's face and smack a noisy kiss on it. "You brute. I'm so happy for you!"

"That makes two of us." He smirks, and Gina laughs and elbows him. He playfully elbows her back, starts the car, and then we're pulling into traffic.

I reach out and make Gina show me the ring. I've always wanted a classy engagement ring—round, with no little sister or brother diamonds anywhere, just the main deal in all its blingy glory. "Ohmygoodness! It's huge on you."

"It's flawless too. Like my girl," Tahoe boasts.

Gina snickers. "Let's just say it's the *only* thing flawless about me."

He takes her hand and kisses it near the ring and I feel a pang of something. My brother is getting *married* even though I was sure he'd never commit to anyone again up to his dying breath.

I suppose I *do* have a romantic side. I see couples who love each other walking down the sidewalk, or holding hands across a table, and something in me yearns. When my brother playfully tugs on Gina's hair, I get warm inside. Even when my dad still does stuff for my mom, like cook her breakfast when she sleeps late, I melt. But I'm smart enough to know relationships like that are an exception, not the rule.

We head into the upscale Gold Coast neighborhood, and although I've heard it equates to the Upper East Side of Manhattan in terms of luxury, my mouth drops when my brother pulls up to a huge wrought-iron gate and waves at the guard.

We're allowed inside and drive up to a sprawling white mansion that's about as contemporary as contemporary gets. My modern-loving heart starts whizzing happily as I take in the expansive windows and the double steel doors. We walk up a set of limestone steps and then enter the modern *Architectural Digest* paradise.

Circular chandeliers made from some invisible material that allows a glimpse of the lights inside hang from thick, dark wood rafters, and strategically placed warm yellow lights illuminate a living room the size of Carma's lobby. But while Carma's lobby is always at 10 percent capacity, this place is packed. The huge windows at the far end of the living room have a view of an endless terrace and several leather-upholstered lounge areas outside. I see the place is scattered with white roses in vases set at intervals across the low, modern glass tables, and I hear Tahoe tell Gina, "Those are all for you."

I feel another pang as their friends yell and clap when they spot them. They start congratulating both of them. I'm introduced to Malcolm Saint, Rachel's husband—my brother's *other* best friend.

"So you're Livvy," he says with a sparkle in his green eyes.

"The very one." I grin back.

I listen to the story of how Tahoe proposed at Navy Pier, by the water, just the two of them there, by putting the engagement ring in a bottle of beer. Music plays in the background and I snag a glass of wine from one of the passing waiters.

Tahoe and Gina look comfortable and happy. I start to wander around the house, loving the bronze sculptures and guessing the artist—Anish Kapoor?—when I hear his voice behind me.

"You fucking loser, come here."

I tense and turn around but I really don't think I was ready to see him, no matter how much I told myself I was as I dressed for tonight.

He sounds both happy and irreverent as he hugs Tahoe and slaps his back with three loud thumps.

I feel my stomach shudder and my spine shoot up straighter as he congratulates Gina and his eyes sort of trail past her shoulder to find me.

I swallow.

"Callan!" A short brunette waves at him as she walks inside, and then she hurries over to say hello.

He leans down to kiss her on the cheek, his hands on her waist, and she turns her head and tries to kiss him on the mouth, but he lifts his head and tells her something and starts toward me.

I look away and try to wade through the crowd.

I spot Wynn sitting with a drink and contemplating the liquid, and my heart sinks when I think of how difficult it must be for her to know that both her best friends will be married before the year ends.

I drop down beside her. I steal a glance in his direction when he's not looking and thank god someone else seems to have stopped him in his tracks. I look at the way he stands, the way he laughs, everything he does is with a masculine sensuality that tugs at me in some primal way.

That girl is hanging onto his side like it's her place. All the chemistry I feel toward Callan instantly goes in the opposite direction with her.

They're flirting I think because she looks dopey-eyed at him, but he appears cool and collected glancing past her shoulder.

And straight at me.

His stare hits me like a lightning bolt.

I glance away.

Wynn jerks her head in the direction of Callan. "What's up with him anyway?"

"What do you mean?"

"Well he's got some willing little friend hanging right by him, and he won't take his eyes off you."

I don't dare turn. I shrug in my best attempt at nonchalance. "I work for him, he's probably uncomfortable that he can't be as bad as he likes because I'm here," I say playfully.

I feel him glance in my direction, and for some reason my eyes feel magnetized to his.

He stands there as if he knows he is good looking times a thousand.

He casts a glance at my little outfit.

We exchange a subtle look that may not be so subtle at all. For a long moment I study his face without hurry, feature by feature. His eyes drink me up too.

And suddenly I can't stand the intensity of his stare, even from across the room.

I excuse myself and wander down a hall, just looking for a little place here that doesn't have him in it.

"Livvy."

I keep walking and hear his footsteps come closer. I open the next door frantically and find myself staring into a utility closet, and as I realize it's the wrong door, he takes my wrist and pulls me inside.

His warm gold-bronze eyes are full of expectation. "Were you not going to say hello?"

"Not really."

He just smiles and crosses his arms and rocks back on his heels, his eyes scanning my getup. "Gold, huh?"

There's a teasing light in his hazel eyes, unmistakable.

"I have a rather boring corporate life, I live for the weekends."

"And I live to see you in that little outfit."

Something fizzles warmly inside my stomach at his words. "Please save your antics."

"It's a compliment." A thoughtful smile curves his lips; he chucks my chin. "If you got them more often you might recognize one."

Nervous by his teasing, I move a step back and bump into a bunch of shelves.

He surveys me in silence, voice low. "Will you be home later tonight?"

"Yes, but not for you."

"I'd like to talk."

"Talk to the tart you're with."

"That *tart* is a good friend of mine and heiress to the Darhausen Wine dynasty."

"There are tarts in every tier of life. Yours happens to be wearing real diamonds, though not much else. She's practically naked in someone's living room."

"It's *my* living room. And I know naked, and that's not it," he says with a seductive crinkle of his eyes, taking a step forward.

This is *his* home?

Shocked, I turn and he touches my shoulder, the warmth of his fingertips on my bare skin startling me. Nearly whimpering, I spin away to avoid the contact.

"Tell me what's on your mind."

I exhale.

"Talk to me."

"I'm embarrassed."

"Why."

"I danced for you."

"You dance very well."

"And I seduced you."

"I know. I was there."

"And you *let* me."

"I did," he agrees, planting a hand next to me on the wall, leaning closer. "I'm glad I'm the one you seduced and not some intern."

"You're not the guy I meant to seduce! I was seducing Derek!"

"Drake."

"Aha." I nod, hating the butterflies I feel when he looks down at me. "Anyone but you."

"That's not true. It was my tongue in your mouth last night, and it was you moaning like crazy when I put it there."

"It shouldn't have been there."

"I say it should've. And so did your moans."

"Those were for Drake."

"Derek." His eyes sparkle in amusement, and more butterflies appear.

I purse my lips to keep from saying anything else.

"Hey," he says, roughly and with unexpected sweetness, "I'm still the same guy you were with last night."

"No, you're not." I scowl. "You led me on. You were *amused* about it." I want to cry.

"I find myself constantly amused by you, I plead guilty to that." He's speaking so sweetly to me I'm only getting sentimental about it.

"Thanks. You should've told me I was hired to be your own personal clown."

"You're not my clown."

"I'm not anything of yours. I just work for you." I shake my head and swallow the lump in my throat. "I thought we were friends. Turns out our friendship was as fake as . . . this ring. As fake as my job at your company."

He has a thousand friends out there. I mean, why would he want to hang out with the twenty-two-year-old little sister of one of his best friends?

"Your brother asked me for a favor, true," he agrees, frowning at my words now, "but I'm not running a charity here. I looked at your résumé. You're well qualified, a little rebellious and with a mind of your own. I appreciate that. And while Roth asked me for a favor, I plan to live up to my side."

"I'm not some sort of tool for you to feel better about yourself," I resentfully say.

"No, you're not. And I would feel better if those blue eyes would stop shooting bullets at me. I enjoy the way you treated me, how real you were with me. I don't get that a lot." He shifts forward, his gaze completely honest and open and oh so warm as he seizes my chin and forces me to meet his gaze. "So I prolonged the time you wouldn't know. And I wanted you last night. And I still want you now."

I drop my gaze to his throat.

The air starts to feel thick enough that my lungs strain for oxygen. Callan and I are absolutely still, me staring at his neck yet achingly aware of his stare fixed on me.

I go through the conversations we shared and feel more and more like a stupid girl with a crush on the guy who wouldn't give her the time of day. The notorious womanizer everybody knows . . . seduced by drunk little me.

"Will you fucking look at me, Olivia?" he growls softly.

My eyes fly up to his. Oh god, he looks frustrated. He sounded frustrated. He said "fucking."

I'm fucking shocked! For a man who exudes so much control, yeah, it's fucking shocking.

He clenches his jaw, then reaches out and grabs my hand, yanking the door open with the other.

"Let's take this outside."

My eyes widen as he leads me down the hall, his hand warm on mine, and I know I should pry it away, but I can't.

We step outside, onto a huge terrace with garden views as far as the eye can see.

He leads me to a lounge and tugs me down to sit next to him, and only then releases my hand. He's staring at me, and I am staring at the expanse of skin revealed by the undone top buttons of his shirt.

It feels like we're back in our own little world, but not quite.

I don't know what to do with my freed hand all of a sudden, curling my fingers into my palm because it tingles. Because his touch lingers.

He continues staring at my profile in quiet desire for something. What, I don't know.

I look at him, and he looks at me, lifting his brow.

He looks at me so piercingly I have no choice but to look back.

"So did you go? See the sights?" He shifts forward, his voice soft, barely audible in the wind.

"I went to the Art Institute. I still want to see so much more. I haven't been out of Texas all that much. My fear of heights gives me panic attacks just thinking about flying. I can only seem to fly on my brother's . . . well."

I shrug, searching for the words.

"Even though I know I'll be okay, physically my body reacts in panic," I finish.

The attentiveness in his eyes, the way he listens, it's hard not to notice. "What happened?" he asks.

"So, we had this tree house when we were little. I think . . ." I hesitate in continuing, but one look into his eyes and I'm done for. I add, "I think we should have a cigarette."

He laughs and pulls one out, lights it, and we share it as I go on. "My brother built it, but he outgrew it by the time he finished, so I claimed it as mine and showed it off to my friends. One day, Jeremy Seinfield came over and tried to kiss me. I told him we were just friends, but he got very mad." I start to laugh as I remember his red, angry face and how scared I was. "He thought I'd invited him to the tree house so we could make out. He got down and demanded I come down too, but since he was yelling and I was afraid, I told him to leave. He pulled the ladder away, and at first, I thought it was a joke and that he'd come back."

I stop laughing and swallow, and he hands me the cigarette, his eyes glimmering in amusement as I take a drag for strength and hand it back.

"My parents were away and my brother had just gotten his first car, a Jeep. He was out with his friends and I was up there all alone, stranded until he got home and heard me crying. I wailed so much I had a sore throat for days. He told me it would be over in a second, and he got a ladder and pulled me down. I didn't want him to let go. Ever." I laugh again at how childish I was.

He chuckles too, but it's a tender laugh, kind of like the one Tahoe has when he remembers that episode, then Callan sobers. "I'm sorry. I hope he sent Jeremy's teeth flying to the other side of the sidewalk."

"Oh, he did." I laugh. "I guess we all have our thing." I eye him. "What's yours?"

"I have a few," he says with that wicked gold sparkle in his eye. "I have an older brother. We'd roughhouse all the time. He was stronger, but I was faster. One day I decided I'd beat him. I started lifting weights, drinking protein shakes, the works, thinking getting stronger was the trick. He beat the shit out of me. And I wasn't fast enough anymore to get away." He laughs. "Not always the strongest win. I decided I'd rather be fast."

"Speaking of slow, I can't believe how slow I was catching on to who you were."

"Slowest woman I've ever met."

"Don't forget my bunch of freckles. That makes me unique."

"Utterly."

We laugh. His lips are so beautiful, more so when he laughs. "Well," I hedge, intending to leave.

"Tell me your concerns about what's happening between us," he says, stopping me in my thoughts.

My eyes widen with dread.

"I don't regret it," he tells me.

I exhale.

"Do you?" he asks.

"Me?"

"Regret last night," he repeats; a question.

I don't think he's breathing as he waits for my reply.

I know that I'm not.

I swallow. This can go nowhere, Olivia, really it can't. I should give him a speech about how wrong this is, how this can't be, but how can I when it feels so right when I'm with him?

I'm not sure if I end up nodding in answer or shaking my head, or a little of both. "I'm confused. I don't know why you even gave me the time of day since that first day on the terrace."

"I like talking to you, Olivia. Is that a crime?" he asks with a soft grin. "Because if it is, I should do it more often."

I sit tight, aware of the excited nerves going through me at his words. God help me. I look away.

"I like looking at you too," he says, just as soft.

My eyes flick up to his. "Because I'm real with you?"

His mouth curves and his eyes quietly promise, *and more.*

I tip my chin up at a haughty angle. "I would've been different if I'd known who you were," I warn.

"That's a shame." He turns very thoughtful and slowly crosses his arms. "That's disappointing, actually."

"Why?"

"Because I like the girl I met on the terrace. The one who danced for me and seduced me to the point I lost control."

I blush. "I'm the same girl. I'm just intimidated."

His full, masculine laugh fills the silence. "Why?"

"I hear things."

"Like what?"

"You're this player. I didn't know I was sleeping with someone who had . . . so much experience. And you're my boss."

"Not your direct boss," he says with a significant rise of his brows. "And so I've played the field all my life, I'm not looking for anything serious. You said yourself, neither were you. Not until . . . what was it?"

"Twenty-eight."

He grins. "Twenty-eight."

"But see, the point is, I have to make it to twenty-eight unscarred," I say. "And a guy like you wouldn't go by without leaving marks along the way."

"How would you know?"

"Because you already did. Last night."

His jaw tenses visibly and his eyes flash with pain by my admission. He raises his arm as he looks at me with tenderness, and then he slowly lowers his hand, as if opting not to touch me. "I'm sorry," he says.

"Callan!" someone calls from inside.

The lines of concentration deepen around his eyes and mouth, and a shadow of disappointment crosses his face as he glances at the door. "I better go."

I nod.

A glint of hesitation appears in his eyes as he rises to his feet. "Are you still up for sightseeing?"

"Always."

He looks at me with a tender smile then clenches his jaw as if refraining from saying something else.

My lids slide down over my eyes, and when I raise them again, I find Callan watching me.

The gold shades in his eyes flicker as if he's battling something, those hazel eyes trapping me. "Where are you planning to go?"

"Millennium Park. Navy Pier." I shrug. "I was going to ask one of the interns, Jeanine or George, if they wanted to come."

"Looking forward to the Ferris wheel at the Pier?"

"Oh, of course, you know how much I adore heights." I laugh.

He laughs too, then turns to me. "I'll take you somewhere."

"No. Please don't. Really. We're good. We'll have a cigarette before I go back home."

He frowns momentarily at my words, staring at me as if seeing me for the first time, here, on his home terrace. The air feels charged. Charged with . . . I don't know.

I want to kiss him.

I don't *want* to want to kiss him.

It feels like goodbye.

I'm not ready to let go of him yet.

But I do. I smile weakly but hope it comes out bright and cheery and he gives me a long look before he walks back inside.

I remain outside for a minute then I head back in as well. I sit with Gina and Rachel, and two more girls who I don't know join us on the couches and start talking about who's dating who, the upcoming wedding, etcetera.

"So are you two planning the wedding of the year?"

"Not at all. We're aiming for something small, either here or in Texas."

I sip on a martini and I peer through the crowd and spot him with a group of guys, his throat kind of sexy as he laughs, thick tendons rippling.

Some girl taps his shoulder, and she looks googly-eyed at him but he nods absently to whatever she asks.

She lifts her hand and offers him her cigarette, and he takes a drag and lets out a slow puff of smoke. I feel an awful pang seeing him share a cigarette with someone else. He shoves it into his mouth and walks over to the bar to mix up a drink, the cigarette dangling from his lips, his eyebrows creased in concentration.

The brunette follows and keeps talking to him, and I see his mouth twist into a smile, even if the cigarette is still there. I look away. Determined to forget him.

I spend Sunday reporting back home:

Mom and Dad (thrilled about the upcoming wedding).

Farrah and Veronica (they want to know how the Chicago clubs compare to the San Antonio and Austin ones).

And then I dial my grandma (she was just happy I called).

Later, I clean the apartment, then I head out to Millennium Park for a run. I run until my throat burns and I'm out of breath, panting with my hands on my knees. Then I drop onto a bench and listen to music as I guzzle down my water, my ponytail wet behind me, my running clothes plastered to my skin as I pull out my cell phone and ask Wynn if she'd like to sightsee and go to the Navy Pier with me.

WORK, WORK, WORK

Wynn told me she saw us talking on the terrace of his place. "Anything going on?" she asked as we walked along the bustling main corridor of the Pier.

"Yes. No." I sighed. "I don't know."

Wynn's advice was *don't go there*.

She immediately grabbed my hand and took me to the bathrooms at the Pier and said, "Let's see . . . aha!" She pointed at some scribbles on the wall and my gaze focused on one that read,

Callan Carmichael is the worst kind of WOMANIZ-ER!!

"He's the last man standing of the three, Livvy. Really, you don't want to go there."

My mouth was hanging open. I was so affronted I even dug out my lipstick and crossed it out.

"Fucking skanks," I cursed as I buried his name under my lipstick.

"Are you siding with him?"

"Yes, I am."

"Shit." She groans. "Callan is a bad boy through and through; he's holding court now as the hottest, richest bachelor in the city."

"I won't go there. I can't help being attracted but I'm not some animal ruled by lust and stuff. I can control it," I assured. "Still. He's my . . . friend. He bailed your ass the other day, Wynn; you can't tell me you don't think he's worth it."

"He's totally worth it. I'm just saying there's no way that man can be tamed."

"Don't worry, this girl isn't in the market," I assured her with false confidence.

The next week, I keep my head down, dive with gusto into everything that Mr. Lincoln needs, and stop going to the terrace. But it's such a hard feat to pretend Callan's not on Earth when he owns the company where I work.

I'm heading home well after 6 p.m. when the elevator down to the lobby opens and a tall man in a black shirt and jeans stands in the middle of two executives.

I feel my stomach clutch uncomfortably even before I really realize it's him. Eyes that change in shades from honey to amber to gold spot me the second I spot him.

His eyes linger a little too long on mine.

I look away, past his shoulders, and board.

The elevator stops on the seventeenth floor, and two more people join us. A protective hand presses me closer to him. Jolting at the touch, I open my mouth to protest but he looks down at me and my voice sort of goes.

"Mr. Carmichael," I say, all professional, once we reach the lobby.

"Livvy," is his only response, half professional and half amused.

I step outside and hurry home.

I bump into him two times more.

Once in the cafeteria. Eating with one of his board members, Malcolm Saint, occasionally lifting his eyes to glance in my direction. I know that he and Malcolm and my brother are good friends, and I wonder if he's the sort of guy who would talk to his friends about me.

Considering I'm Tahoe's sister—not *likely*.

The second time, I'm exiting the revolving doors of the building. I stop and glance up the length of the building as if I could see him on the terrace.

He steps outside the very same instant and catches me staring up, and he smiles a little and just says, "Livvy."

"Mr. Carmichael."

God, would the floor open up and eat me now already?

That Friday, when he enters the cafeteria it feels like there's a shift in energy in the room.

"Carmichael gets my heart pounding when he walks in," Janine says, giggling over her lunch as we sit together in the west wing of the cafeteria.

Carrie, another intern, glances his way. "He's all you see, isn't he? It's impossible not to notice him."

I shuffle through the notes in my current research project folder.

"Except Livvy, she's too busy." Carrie grins and plays with her straw.

I smile, because I'm not sure what else to do.

But I won't look at him.

Hurrying to finish my lunch, I head back up to continue assisting Mr. Lincoln organize his next proposal.

We stay late for an extra hour as he reviews some notes he brought back from the executive floor. He's been studying iBots, an app company based in Los Angeles that's in Callan's razor eye for his next takeover.

I'm engrossed with all the details as I type up Lincoln's corrections when the phone rings. I absently lift the receiver and recite the usual greeting. "Carma Inc. Henry Lincoln's office."

"Miss Olivia Roth? This is Ivonne Miller, Mr. Carmichael's assistant. Mr. Carmichael would like to see you in his office right away."

I almost choke on my own saliva.

I gulp out a "yes" and then try to plead for the floor to swallow me whole before I need to go upstairs.

It doesn't.

I tap on Mr. Lincoln's door. "Mr. Lincoln, Mr. Carmichael asked to see me, but if there's anything you need, anything at all, I'd be happy to let his assistant know—"

"Callan?" His head jerks away from his computer screen. "Absolutely, go. Nothing here worth declining this . . . unexpected interest. Go right on, missy! Shoo." He waves me off, laughing when I start to flush because obviously I don't want to go.

"Livvy." He stops me at the door. "He's not as bad as they say he is."

I gulp. "That doesn't give me any relief, sir." I nod, but turn around and head to the elevators.

My knees feel wobbly as I step inside the elevator and look at my reflection.

Is it wrong that I worry about how I look?

I'm wearing the black-and-white uniform. Black skirt, a short white jacket. Black pumps. My hair in a braid down my back. I look as if I fit here, even though every hour of the day —hell, since I got here—I wonder if I do.

Everyone here has a big ego. As if working for Carmichael makes them superior to the rest of humanity. Except I don't get to feel that way because I'm only here thanks to . . . well, Tahoe. I can't kid myself about that.

The doors open on the top floor, right below the building terrace. A desk greets me, and a beautiful middle-aged woman with a dark bun stands and calls my name. "Miss Roth?"

She has a small pregnant belly and manages to make it look as if carrying a child and working full time is as natural as breathing.

I nod and smile at her.

"Go right in." She clicks a button on the desk and a beeping sound comes from the shiny silver doors as they roll open.

I walk inside.

He's already on his feet, like all the times I found him on the terrace, as if he's waiting for me.

Our eyes meet, and that name echoes through my body like a little earthquake starting in the center of my chest and amplifying outward like a ripple.

Callan.

"Livvy." His voice sounds gravelly as he shoves his hand in his pocket and watches me walk forward.

I feel awkward.

I miss my mailman. He looks so intimidating right now. I tug on my skirt and jacket and go drop down on one of the two chairs in front of a huge modern desk.

His office is eternal, never-ending, three walls of floor-to-ceiling windows. The wall next to the doors has the biggest screen I've ever seen, composed of dozens and dozens of small screens, ticking with stock numbers and Bloomberg news.

He doesn't take the seat behind his desk. Instead, he leans his arms against the chair and stands behind it, looking at me with a devilish grin. "I assumed you'd appear in a red dress to test me."

"Somebody should. You wear what you like, but every employee here can't. It's not fair."

"Life's not fair." He walks around the chair and finally drops down, leaning back and crossing his arms behind his head. "I've learned the value in discipline to get me right where I am, on the top floor and a few steps ahead of the pack."

He's so hot.

And very unscrupulous, Olivia!

And your boss.

I don't want to think of how much I miss the twinkle in his eye or the way he used to smile in amusement at me.

Or the way he felt when he moved inside me.

We both stare from opposite sides of the desk and I wonder if he's thinking about it too. Even the way he sleepy-fucked me.

"Lincoln tells me the Alcore proposal was your idea."

My eyes widen in surprise. "I wasn't expecting him to send it over. I just e-mailed it Sunday."

"Well, he did. And I'm impressed."

Despite myself, my heart does a little leap of joy.

"He's pleased with your work," Callan says.

"Thank you."

"So I've been putting some thought into this." His chair creaks as he shifts and strokes his chin with his thumb. "Tahoe asked me to take you under my wing at Carma, said that you wanted to learn. And I think the best way for you to do that is to finish your internship as my assistant."

I'm shocked into silence. Confused at first, then scared, then a little flattered.

He explains, "Ivonne is taking her maternity leave early, and I'd really like you to step up and step in."

A thousand nervous little pricks run inside my body. I shift restlessly in my chair. "Well I don't know that I want to leave Mr. Lincoln."

"You don't want to leave Mr. Lincoln," he repeats.

"It's just that he's very disorganized on his own. He needs someone to help him organize his thoughts," I explain.

He looks vaguely amused for a second then deeply frustrated the next. Finally he seems amused again, and he adds, "I will be sure that Mr. Lincoln has someone very capable of helping him organize his thoughts."

His eyebrows rise as he waits for me to say more.

Obviously he expects me to say *yes*. Maybe even do a happy dance right here in my chair. But the mere thought of being close to him makes me uneasy. Something tells me Callan is going to push me to my limits.

I know down to my bones it won't be easy with Callan Carmichael at all.

Because he's so goal-oriented and so cold in his business dealings.

And also because deep beneath that hot designer suit, there's still that very real human guy I had sex with, and that might be the most disadvantageous thing of all. I have a freaking soft spot for that guy, my mail guy. I opened up to him, I . . . *wanted* him. And he's not the guy I thought he was.

This second, as I look at the guy across the desk from me in a white shirt and gray slacks, his handsome face reserved, I feel only confusion because I want to open up to him again, and at the same time, I want to run as fast and far away from him as my legs and these slick corporate heels will take me.

"Why do you do this?" I ask him, pointing at the stock tickers on the screen.

"Why do *you*?" he counters.

"Tahoe is the one who made me so interested in business. My family wasn't always rich. My parents were struggling, and Tahoe was always working at the oil rigs, until he met a guy with a struggling oil lease, and he invested the little he had, bought his first lease and rig, and helped the man out. Three years later he'd struck a gold mine, made his partner rich, and became independent on his own.

"I saw what he did for my parents, giving them a sense of financial security they'd never had. It intrigued me and made me want to do the same, not for me or my family, since we're taken care of, but for others. Finding ways to bring their businesses back to a full working state."

"And I do this because I'm good at it. I'm the best at it. FYI."

I roll my eyes. "You're so cocky it's almost sexy."

His eyes glint playfully. "Almost?"

I frown. "Almost."

He grins back at me. "Do I get a yes now, as I am *almost* sexy when I'm cocky? I can be very persuasive too," he says.

I wait.

He leans forward on his desk. "You're so blunt it's almost insanely attractive."

"Almost?"

He nods. "Almost."

His eyes darken as soon as he says that, and we both stop smiling when we realize we were *flirting.*

His office could've just fallen away, and we could've been up on that terrace again, nothing but a guy and a girl and that's it.

He grins sardonically. "I expected you'd say yes, Livvy." He raises a challenging brow and looks at me with the same eyes my Hot Smoker Guy used to look at me.

And because of the guy I met on the terrace, because I want to be honest with *that* guy, I tell him the truth.

"I . . . thank you, but I'm not sure that's a good idea." I hesitate before saying the rest, but he seems to read my mind. We were just *flirting* after all. Oh god. This is *not* good! "After what happened—"

He cuts me off. "I told your brother I'd help, and I want to come through. I told him you'd learn here, and I think the best way for you to do that is to be my assistant."

He leans back and studies me.

Of course he doesn't miss the fact that I still haven't said yes.

There's an intimacy in the room—something warm in his eyes. Something warm inside me that I'm struggling to cool down.

"I was hoping you weren't asking me for my brother."

"I'm not." Calmly, he says, "When I started working at my father's firm, my father put me through the wringer to get me where I am today. I worked twelve-hour days, doing anything I could—anything," he emphasizes. "I couldn't have built Carma without the experience. Someone needs to do the dirty work. I quickly learned none of my employees are willing to do it as effusively as when they know you're willing to do it yourself."

"I want the work," I agree, "but I want to help people too. I don't know that I'll feel comfortable working so closely with you when you specialize in ripping companies apart. I joined the firm thinking I could learn here, but I wanted to remain distant from that aspect of it."

Shadows cross his eyes, and his voice drops a decibel as he leans forward on his desk again. "Is that what you think I do? Just take a bite, chew them up and spit out the pieces, Olivia?" He seems both puzzled and slightly amused. "You clearly don't understand what I do here. You have a lot to learn."

"I know that," I say softly.

"I'm not the devil, Livvy. I just choose to allow some to believe that I am."

He gives me the smile that makes my pulse skip.

"Callan—Mr. Carmichael, you've got the wrong girl. Radisson in Austin didn't even offer an internship. I'm really so green still . . ."

He eyes me with a hint of anger and shifts forward just a bit more. "I trust my own judgment better than anyone else's. Olivia, everyone starts at the bottom. Hell, it's *better* to start at the bottom. Sooner or later we all get acquainted with the ground. Starting from the ground up is what gives you a solid foundation."

Well he's kind of badass, and not in a bad way.

I think my nana would like him.

But she'd call him a scoundrel for sure.

He's so young, it's incredible to think of all the things I know I could learn from this guy. He could teach me. I could learn. At the price of what, though?

I can't even look at him without feeling a big, warm   T I N G L E! Urgh!

"I'm just not sure you've got the right girl," I finally say.

"I'll be the judge of that," he says as he stands and eases his arms into his jacket.

I nod and stand too, following him outside on automatic.

"We're off," he tells his assistant, tapping his knuckles on her desk as we pass. "Go rest."

We ride the elevator, and I eye him, full of regret.

If only he had been seventy-year-old Daniel Radisson. Safe Daniel Radisson who helps businesses like I want to do someday, is supposedly kind and my father's friend instead of my brother's. I would've instantly, immediately said yes from the get-go.

"I'm hungry," he says casually. "You hungry?"

"I . . . yes."

He smiles.

I do anything but look at that hot, sexy smile.

We head down a couple of blocks to a hot dog stand and I regret blurting out that I was hungry.

"Tell me about Radisson."

"I wanted Radisson Investments because they don't make the big kills, it's a company with heart so . . . they invest in struggling companies and sort of salvage some. It's a very prestigious firm in Austin. Not as prestigious as yours but . . . but there's a reason he didn't want me," I insist.

"This Radisson. Does he know you're interning with me?"

"Of course."

We stop to buy hot dogs and I take a bite and savor mine, without ketchup like the Chicagoans had instructed me, then add, "I went to Radisson's office and rubbed it in his face that I got an internship with you." I laugh. "And it felt good!"

I see him reach out as if to touch my face, but I jerk my head nervously and he lowers his hand. "I could eat that business up without blinking and spit out their bones." He smiles and winks at me. His gaze changes when he looks at my lips. "There's something else that needs to be rubbed off."

I lick the mustard off the corner of my lips, but he still reaches out with his thumb to pick up the rest. The sexiest thing I've ever seen a man do could possibly be Callan lifting his thumb and sucking the mustard off it. My lungs feel a little broken in my chest and I feel like grabbing a bottle of mustard and bathing in it so he licks it off me.

This man drives me *insane.*

My hormones insane.

My mind insane.

We're halfway through our hot dogs when I hear a female voice to my left. "Callan!" a woman calls breathlessly.

I wipe my mouth with my napkin as she comes over and Callan sort of boredly watches her. "Olivia," he says, introducing me.

"Oh, hi." The woman looks crestfallen all of a sudden, quickly glancing back at him and pasting a smile on her face.

"My favorite person in the world! We were going to see you at your polo match in two weeks."

"I'll see you there, then."

The girl is so beautiful, with long black hair and eyes. She waits to see if he says something else then, but he doesn't.

I run my hands over my uniform, suddenly self-conscious.

"Well . . . bye." She heads back over to her friend.

I stay quiet and we finish our hot dogs.

I know that if he wanted her, he could have her. Like, right here and now. And it gives me a little pang of jealousy and an urge to erase our night of sex from my memory.

"Do you always get everything you want?" I ask him.

"Everything." He tosses his napkin into the trash, and then does the same with mine. I expect him to say goodbye, but soon we're just walking.

"I know what you're thinking. That I'm being foolish and that I should take the job, but it's best if I stay where I am. I like it where I am."

"That's not what I'm thinking."

We stop walking.

He slips his hand into my hair. "Tell me to kiss you, Livvy."

"Why would I do that?"

"Because you haven't stopped thinking about it."

"I have."

"In that case, I haven't." He strokes a finger down my jaw. "So. How about you kiss me. For my sake."

"Come on. You get kissed all the time, I'm sure."

"Not by you, not nearly enough."

I exhale, leaning against the building behind me for support. We're kind of secluded, at the entrance to an alley. People are passing by on the street, oblivious to us.

"So how about you kiss me like you did that night." He tugs my chin up. "Or let me kiss you like I did that night."

"You kissed me all over."

"Then at least let me kiss those intoxicating lips of yours. For now."

I blink, and I start to shake my head from side to side in *no,* but it's also bobbing up and down in *yes.*

He smiles slowly, seductively, and pulls me to him by the back of the head and suddenly his eyes are darkening.

He smells warm and male and strong.

He leans down. His mouth devours mine softly. I feel his fingers slip into mine as he drags me closer and deeper into the alley. His warm hand slides up my left cheek, and we don't speak, only kiss.

He leans his head and I go up on tiptoe, confused and afraid and still unable to resist him.

His tongue flicks at my lips and then past them, touching mine.

It's wet and warm, gentle and exploratory.

My fingers dig into his shoulders and his hands press me closer.

I'm panting and aching between my legs, rocking my hips slightly to his. It's like my body is begging and he grabs my hips and holds me against him, where he's hard, and grinds us as he gives me another kiss, giving me just a hint of what could be.

Another kiss, this one more sensual, more carnal.

His fingers spread on my cheek as he tips up my face, and his other hand closes around a handful of my hair as he sucks on my tongue.

My heart pounds against my chest, and through the soft cotton of his shirt pressed against my thin satin top, I think I feel his heart too.

We ease apart. His eyes close. I tip my head as our foreheads somehow touch.

I can still taste him in my mouth. It's difficult to pry my eyes open and meet his gaze, but when I do, he's looking down at me with eyes that look very male.

He uses his thumb to tip my head up a notch and force me to hold his gaze. His voice sounds like sand on velvet. "Are you okay with this?"

His textured voice.

His piercing stare.

I want Callan so much, I have to curl my fingers into my palms to keep them from plunging into that wind-blown hair, pulling his head down to mine, touching his lips again, feeling him taste me with all that lusty hunger again.

I laugh nervously.

One second I'm laughing, the next my breath stops as his lips brush over mine again. "Say you're okay with this."

I gasp, the lightning-bolt feeling of his kiss coming back. And his hand slides from my cheek to grip my hair again, while his other hand joins it on my scalp, holding me in place as he angles his head and parts my lips open for him. He does it firmly, hungrily, as if he can't control himself, as if he needs this for some reason.

All I'm aware of is the slick heat of his mouth, the rush in my blood as I move my mouth just as fast as he does. My hands slide into his hair, gripping, and he groans as if he likes the response. Callan's groan makes me ache in places.

He cups my face in his warm hands as he peels his lips away, breathing harshly. "Say it, Olivia. That you want my kiss all over, under this," he tugs my top, "below your waist . . ."

I'm dizzy. He makes it so hard to think straight and even harder to make me even want to try to pull away. His arms feel so amazingly, incredibly good as he slides them to my waist, keeping us flush.

"Flirting is just not convenient," I pant.

"I agree it's not." He grins with his lips and with his eyes. "Kissing is really, really pushing it."

I exhale shakily. "Well then, no flirting. No kissing. Especially at the office."

His hands clench convulsively on my hips as if he has no intention of letting me escape.

My body is sort of leaning on his, my arms sort of twisted around his neck as I tip my head up and look into his eyes. "If we have sex again, it'd just be to work each other out of our systems. Only tonight. Monday is Monday and nothing happened. Nothing," I say.

A dark, fierce look appears in his eyes. "It's not Monday yet."

"I want you," he says, cupping my face, kissing me deeper.

I glance at the condom basket tucked under my nightstand. "As you can see, I'm very prepared. Condoms. A lifetime supply."

He shakes his head, *tsk*ing as he brushes my hair behind my face. "That's not a lifetime supply, Olivia."

"Well . . ." I flush. He walks us to the bed and lays me down on it, his slacks half unzipped, his chest bare and glorious.

"I've never had an orgasm with a guy until you," I admit.

He lifts his brows, his smile fading as he eases back to look at me. "Are you serious?"

"I'm always serious. Are you calling me a liar? Why do you look so shocked? I'm not a virgin—you didn't get to pop my cherry."

He's just staring at me.

He smiles again, then his eyes turn smoldering and his smile fades as he looks at me. This raw look crosses his eyes before he leans over and takes my mouth, softly, so softly.

"Oh god, that feels good." I throw my neck back and run my fingers over his bare chest as he tugs my top upward.

He pulls it over my head. I grab his hair as his lips run down my neck.

"Callan," I breathe. I arch my back.

He strokes his hand down my bare torso and abdomen. "I like that," he says. He looks at my mouth for a whole minute, then his hand cups my jaw. His eyes are a mixture of hunger, amusement, and tenderness. He leans over and kisses me, slipping his tongue into my mouth slowly this time, as if I'm irresistible. Meant to be savored.

He unfastens my bra and tugs it off, then rubs the hard point of my nipple with his thumb. I run my fingers down his abs.

Callan is the kind of guy who has perfect genetics, who is muscled naturally, athletic and gifted and gorgeous.

I can feel every one of those muscles under my fingertips right now as I head for his cock.

He groans when I slip my fingers into his slacks and find him hot, so hard against his boxers.

I rub a little, loving when he groans again.

And he kisses me.

He eases his hand into his boxers and pulls out his cock and rubs it against my thigh with a greedy thrust.

Shit! I'm so ready I'm trembling—literally trembling from the heat in my body and the cool air in the room. He pushes his slacks down and then is naked.

"Ohhhhh," I groan, and as a reward, he tongues me.

I drag my bare feet up the back of his calves.

I inhale sharply when he tugs my skirt up my thighs. His fingers edge into my inner thigh, sure and determined.

I rock my hips as his fingertip teases me through my panties.

He's a living, breathing candy and right now he's all for me.

He starts kissing my lips again as he eases his fingers into my panties and starts rubbing my folds. I don't know how to feel, how to react, my world is spinning a thousand miles a minute, there is no bed beneath me, nothing but my arms around his neck, clenching, and his hot mouth, and his expert touch.

His strong hands circle my waist and lift me to sit up on the bed. He tugs my panties off along with my skirt. Says, "I think I should get in here and look for some freckles."

He turns me slightly to look at the back of my shoulders.

The touch of his fingertips against my bare skin feels like the most divine thing in the world. He bends his dark head and takes the back of my neck in his mouth, suckling gently. My body arcs and twists in pleasure. "This is my favorite one," he says as he shifts me slowly around and takes my breast in his mouth. "And this one." He's got me fully facing him now as he takes my other nipple and sucks it even harder.

God, I might not survive tonight but I'll die having an orgasm. Sex has never been like this. I've never been mindless for it—for a guy. For him. I spread my legs open to make room for him and clutch his hair and twine my legs around him.

"Please," I beg.

His voice is thick with desire too. "Olivia, did you mean what you said? No man has ever made you come before?"

Please god, make Callan stop saying the word come.

I struggle with the wave of desire surging through me and arch up against him. "I meant it at the time but that's not the case anymore."

His eyes shine tenderly as he thumbs back a loose strand of hair behind my forehead. "I want to do more things to you. Make you writhe all night. Make you come for all the times a man has touched you and you haven't."

"Okay. Challenge accepted," I pant. "There've been like a hundred men."

"A hundred men?" he repeats, smiling because he knows I'm just being greedy.

I bob my head up and down and bite my lip.

His eyes remain heavy, but his lips curl into a sensual smile as he crawls up to me. "Liar, liar, your tongue's on fire." He licks his tongue into my mouth and slips his hand between my legs.

Bolts of heat shoot from his fingertips slickly caressing my folds and up my whole body. Through the haze of desire coming over me, I absently realize that he's got the best hands in the world and smells the best, feels the best, tastes the best. I've never felt like this.

I never want this moment to end.

I'm on a high I never want to come down from.

I'm flying.

So high, this is dangerous and definitely not good for me —and I still want it. I want more of it, of Callan Bad Boy Carmichael.

He licks my lips. "You're coming so fast, so hard, and so very frequently tonight there won't be a day that you come and not think of me." He licks me again, a flick of his tongue. Warm. Wet.

He plays me with his fingers.

"Open up to me, Olivia," he murmurs into my mouth.

The tip of his cock replaces his fingers.

And I do.

I lie in my bed on Saturday, still buzzing head to toe, my body humming with arousal, my lips tasting of Callan.

My phone rings. I start when I see an unfamiliar number on the screen and quickly pick up, dreading for it to be him. Dreading for it to *not* be him.

He left while I was sleeping.

That can't be good.

I answer but remain silent on the line.

There's a corresponding silence for a moment, then he speaks, and his voice trails over me, so warm and textured, I close my eyes for a moment.

"You have a good time last night?"

"Yes."

"So did I."

I stare out the window. "Really? Why did you leave?"

"I had breakfast with my dad."

"Oh." I swallow. "So this . . . this attraction between us. We can make it go away, right?"

He laughs.

"Callan. I'm going back home soon, I wasn't really looking for anything else. When I seduced you I was buzzed and you were this hot stranger I loved talking to."

"You don't like talking to me now?" There's amusement in his voice and this odd husky tenderness.

"Actually I do," I quickly explain. "But I don't want to be attracted to you. I want to focus on work. No distractions. It seemed a good idea to just get each other out of our systems."

"Is it working for you?" he asks.

"I don't know."

"Let me know when you do."

"Okay."

"Good night, freckles."

"Good night, Callan."

I hang up and stare at the phone. Freckles? What does it mean? Does it mean we'll go on? No. There is *no* way we can go on. I text him early the next morning after a sleepless night.

No regrets, but tomorrow you're Mr. Carmichael. And that's what you'll be from now on.

I'll see you tomorrow.
Miss Roth.

CLUB

The next weekend, the interns are ready for our night out, and I'm ready for fun. I'm all dressed up in a skimpy, cute little black dress, red heels, a long, simple gold necklace and a pair of bangles, my hair loose.

"I'm so ready to dance!" I say. I want to forget Callan and dance my sexual frustration away.

"Change of plans. George's brother can get us into Havoc, a very exclusive club only the VIPs of the city go to, mostly all single." Janine wiggles her brows as we ride a cab toward the club.

"Just give me a song and a dance floor. And a drink," I say.

"I'll dance with you," says George.

"Thanks, George." Then I notice Janine doesn't look too pleased about it.

We hop out of the cab. The driveway outside the club is lined with fancy cars.

There, among the long line, is my brother's Rolls-Royce Ghost.

God. Really? Fuck! I panic. "Wait!" I grab Janine by the arm.

"A problem, Roth?" George asks me.

I hesitate, then exhale. I don't want my brother to be disappointed, but I'm sure he doesn't want me at the clubs just for my protection, not because he doesn't want me to have fun. Plus I'm feeling homesick. I've never slept in an empty apartment. I've always lived with my parents before. And I don't want to think of freaking Callan.

I shake my head. It's a big city, and a big club, and I'll just find my own little corner of it to dance in.

Once we're let inside by the bouncer after George tells him his brother's name, I scan the crowd and see Tahoe is standing by a group that's sitting in a booth. He glances at his watch as Regina hugs one of the girls goodbye, then wraps an arm around her waist and leads her away.

I exhale, give a little prayer of thanks, then I scan the crowd again.

A man with dark hair shifts in the booth and *there* is the anonymous man of my wet dreams, the one who'd never had a face before Callan.

Some girl is hovering over him and I feel a pang of jealousy. Really, she's welcome to all his cigarettes, thank you. I could use the extra minutes of life.

I head to the opposite corner of the club and Janine follows as she skims the hot guys available. "Table or mingle?"

"Dance," George says, and he takes my hand.

"Drinks first," I tell George.

Armed with our cocktails of choice, we end up on a spacious floor under flashing strobe lights, mirrored chandeliers, and in between a hundred dancing people. I listen to the music, a wicked song by Adam Lambert, and I move to the rhythm, closing my eyes and sipping my drink.

Chills run down my spine all of a sudden.

I open my eyes and I see, past elbows and shoulders and moving forms, *him* watching me from his table.

I have a sudden image of me dancing for him the first time we had sex, when I didn't know who he was, and I can't stop dancing. I move my hips and hold his copper gaze.

He starts smiling as if to himself and raking me with his eyes, as if he's a biologist studying an animal in a zoo.

I sigh and take a sip of my drink when I realize it's empty already.

He continues watching me with this little smile.

Slowly, he rises and stalks toward me.

Oh. Crap. Shit.

I take George's drink and down it all. He looks shocked. "I like my girl to know how to party. Want me to get us another one?"

"Um, yes, or *several*," I yell out over the noise as he heads for the bar.

I realize he's left me alone on the dance floor while Callan moves through the crowd in my direction. I'm left with nothing to do and nothing to drink but the sensuality of his physique. In a panic, I turn to the couple dancing to my right and begin to sway with them to the sound of "King of Sabotage" by Ferras.

"Olivia," I hear behind my ear.

I hold my breath, but then turn and grin. "Derek."

"Drake."

"Fancy seeing you here, Drake. At this den of iniquity." I signal around said den of iniquity.

"This den is not for little girls."

He grabs my hand like it belongs to him.

And my hand fits right in his like it belongs there.

My eyes widen as he purposely leads me through the crowd, holding my hand the entire time, and I know I should pry it away but I can't. He's staring at me and I am staring at the expanse of skin revealed by the undone top buttons of his shirt.

We step outside, onto a terrace.

He leads me to a sitting area and tugs me down to sit next to him, and only then releases my hand.

I don't know what to do with it all of a sudden, curling my fingers into my palm because it tingles. Because his touch lingers.

He continues staring at my profile in quiet desire for something. What, I don't know.

I'd say sex, but I already had that with him.

I look at him, and he looks at me, lifting his brow.

He looks at me so piercingly I have no choice but to look back.

My eyes dart around the room restlessly. "I don't want my friends to see me with you."

"Why?"

"Because they're my coworkers and you're the boss."

"Not your direct boss."

"We're interns, that's like a whole different caste system. I want to make friends while I'm here. In case you haven't realized, a lot of people are scared shitless of you at Carma."

He lifts a brow.

I reach into his shirt pocket and pull out a lighter and a cigarette.

"Why haven't you come to the terrace?" he asks as he watches me light up. He also sounds displeased.

"You went to the terrace?" I counter.

"I always go the terrace. Why would I stop going? It's my terrace, Olivia," he murmurs. He's watching me intently.

"I had work to do . . ." Then I smile. "Wow, you noticed," I say, exaggerating his smarts.

There's a twitch to his lips. "Barely. You hardly talk—so you can understand why it would be hard for me to notice."

The word *hard* rolls off his tongue rather too sexily.

I frown. Callan rests his chin on his hand and scrapes his thumb along the line of his jaw thoughtfully as he studies me. "Are you avoiding me?" He sounds bossy now. He edges closer, his shoulder close to mine, his eyes smiling but curious. "Did I grow fangs and an appetite for the blood of girls with secret *clusters* of freckles?" he asks.

"Well, you did show me your appetite is rather hefty."

"I'm not the only one with a hefty appetite. You couldn't take me inside you fast enough the other day."

I open my mouth and can't even think of what to say.

"Look this can't happen," I finally say when I recover. "My brother will kill us."

"What the devil doesn't know can't hurt him." He leans in and licks inside my lips.

Everything no man has made me feel, this one does. I'm crackling like a raw wire, torn to the fringes, explosion-ready. "You're shameless."

"I am."

"Reckless and irreverent!"

"Yep." He smiles. "I just want to get to know you, Olivia," he whispers in my ear, then he looks at me, his eyes heavy-lidded. "I want more of this." He licks into my lips again and holds the back of my head as he parts my mouth with his.

"I don't know when you're teasing and when you're not," I whisper, slipping my fingers into his hair.

God! I missed him.

"Then you better get to know me too." He grins, then he cups the back of my head so gently you'd think I was made of crystal.

He kisses me, softly this time, carefully. I melt into his kiss, scratching my nails against the back of his neck. I groan from the pleasure.

"You're so fascinating, Livvy." He smiles as he withdraws, and he looks at me so tenderly, as if he wants to protect me.

"Callan . . ." I begin, unsure of what to say.

He seems to sense my fear and he lets me go. He pulls out a cigarette now and lights up, and I look at it yearningly as he offers it to me.

I shake my head. Nope. I do not want to smoke from his cigarette. Just watching him do that soft sucking motion to the end of his cigarette makes me sweat. I'm already soaked between my legs and ready to beg him to put his finger inside me.

Callan hasn't even taken a second drag when I stand to leave. "I need to go back to my friends before they see me with you."

He stands and puts out his cigarette then he shoves his hands into his pockets as I head to the doors. "Livvy," he says.

I turn, and the wind is in his hair the way I want my fingers to be. The wind pushes his button shirt against his chest and his slacks against his long, muscled legs.

"I'll take you home."

I groan at how stubborn he sounds. "You took me to the ball twice already, Callan, thank you." I turn back again.

"Come here," he says, his voice stopping me.

"Excuse me?"

He sighs and drags a hand over his hair. He stretches out a lovely muscular arm with short blond hairs, his palm up, and wiggles his fingers, a little exasperated. "Come here. Give me your phone."

I frown but obey.

"Text me when you get home."

He types something on the phone.

"I'm not going to text you," I protest as I take back my phone.

"You're going to text me or you're leaving right now with me." He nods like there's no doubt about him getting his way.

"I'll text you," I quickly agree and head inside, telling myself I won't call him, hating the grin I saw appear when I hastily agreed.

I tell my friends I'm heading home early and take an Uber. When I'm back in the apartment, I brush my teeth and get ready for bed and tell myself I can't let that personal connection and easy conversation happen again. I want to avoid calling him but here I am, scanning my contacts.

I find his number stored under **Not Drake.**

I smile over the fact that I had stored him, previously, as **Derek.** Checking my smile, I frown and type.

I'm home. Satisfied?

For now.

Where are YOU?

Home. Getting some work done.

Oh really? Wow. Well so am I, I lie and get my laptop out, my competitive side stirred.

Such a hard little worker. Lucky boss.

He's a bit of a hard one too, I text.

There's a silence and my eyes widen when I realize what I said.

Yes.
He IS.

My tummy flutters.
Oh lord above, help me.
I drop my phone as if it singed me and then power it off.
Olivia Roth? His antics cannot get to you. It is not allowed.

I try to quell what seeing him tonight did to me and blame it on the alcohol I imbibed.

Because that crush has been crushed. I'm no longer a naïve young girl needing her brother to bail her out when she gets in trouble, hell, I'm a full-time working girl and I can't be Callan's shiny new toy.

I'm worth more than that even though I've always battled with feelings of not being enough. Isn't that why I'm so desperate to prove myself?

Too many people labeling me a blonde bimbo. Too many people underestimating me until I've almost believed they're right.

In that sense only my brother believed in me—and no matter how much I've idolized my father's old friend Daniel Radisson all this time, it was bad boy Callan Carmichael who gave me a chance.

I'm determined to use it and focus on what's important to me.

Maybe if I stopped feeling prejudiced against Callan's business ruthlessness, I could pull my head out of my ass and ask him to teach me.

Janine is now interning with Callan and lunches are proving difficult when I have to listen to her gush on how hot he is and how intensely she's learning. She also mentions she picks up regular calls for him from a thousand and one girls, all asking if he's in, for Janine to *please* ask him to call them, inquiring about whether he got this or that invitation, etcetera.

Etcetera.

Etcete-fucking-ra.

"I'm seriously learning so much just by the little glimpses I get into the conference room and phone calls. I won't even say how I'll feel if I manage to get a night with him in my pocket, too, oh god. Livvy, the size of his you-know-what is like . . . you can see the size through his pants. And he's got big hands, obviously it's huge, he has huge shoes too. And that mouth! He's so wicked!" She's flushed as she speaks.

I push the food around my plate, not hungry now. Conversation swirls around us, and all this time, I'm only aware of the low, dull throb inside me.

I came here to work, to learn. Did I let my own personal prejudices and confusing feelings keep me from learning all that I can, from the best man I could possibly learn it from?

I excuse myself and head up to Mr. Lincoln. He's reviewing the research I submitted earlier today, and he looks distracted as he glances at me from across his desk and asks me to pull up the Alcore proposal again. "Callan requested an update."

My heart kicks in excitement, and I nod and head to my desk. "Right away, sir."

Later that evening, after a full day of work and trying not to dwell back on the two nights I've spent with the boss— because, really, it needs to stop! There will be no, no third!—I make a phone call to my grandma.

"Hey, Nana!"

"Who is this? Do I know you?"

"You don't just know me, you *adore* me." I curl up on the couch and glance at the steaming green tea I just set on my coffee table—I take it bitter without sweetener, just like my grandmother taught me. "I'm just checking in, Nana. How are you?"

"I'm well, but freaking missing my *favorite* granddaughter!"

"I'm your *only* granddaughter. I freaking miss you too."

I hear her laugh, and then a creak, and I imagine her settling on the swing outside on her front porch. "Tell me about Chicago."

I grin. "It's good." My smile fades a little and I draw an invisible pattern on my jeans. "I just felt a little homesick," I say, then I ask her what she's been up to, just wanting to hear the familiarity of home and the routine I know she follows by memory. Pruning the rosebushes, adding food to the birdhouse on the huge oak outside, baking something to give away, looking at old pictures and living by memories of her time when my dad was young, when my grandfather was alive.

It's familiar, homey, and grounding.

I feel like I need that. Like I climbed a little too far up the Callan Carmichael tree house and I need my family to hold a ladder for me so I can climb back down.

ELEVATOR

I have a restless night. I dream I'm in the tree house, smoking on the ledge, when Jeremy Seinfield tries to kiss me. Except this time I don't turn away. I lean closer and open my mouth, never so eager for him to kiss me before. I slip my hands into his hair and he tastes of coffee and cigarettes. I'm so surprised by how well he kisses, I ease back and stare at him in shock. But it's not Jeremy looking back at me. I look into eyes that are a swirl of bronze, his voice a man's voice, not a boy's.

"I'm Callan."

I wake up Friday morning to my alarm buzzing on my nightstand. I groan and turn around, squinting at the time to realize it's already 7 a.m.

I hurry to start getting ready, moving through the apartment.

It's already familiar, the view outside, my bed. I leave in less than two months, really. It's only a summer internship.

I think of him in my bed and how my sheets still smell of him.

I think of the terrace. All those meetings I won't have again. They're branded in my memory, down to the shirts he wore and the way he smelled. It's not like he's the only good-smelling man out there, but there's something special about his scent. It's familiar, warm, and comforting. His eyes and the way we talk as if we've known each other forever.

No regrets, I remember.

I sigh and go shower and get ready for work. I slip into my Carma uniform and tuck my hair into a neat bun, then look at myself in the mirror. Blonde, blue-eyed, young, and determined—that's what I want my boss to see.

Not naked, moaning, and writhing—that was only for my Hot Smoker Guy to see.

"Hold the elevator," a familiar voice says when I arrive at Carma that morning. I jerk up straighter and my hand starts to tremble slightly as I press the open button.

Callan steps inside, typing something into his phone as he boards, stands beside me, selects his floor, and tucks his phone into his pocket.

He's wearing a suit today and my knees wobble under my skirt.

I'm not sure he's even realized it's me who's standing alone with him in the elevator until he speaks. "How are you?"

Well. Let's see now. I came in this hot guy's arms several times and I can't quite get him off my mind, I think helplessly.

"Great," I say instead. "You?"

"Good now."

Through the corner of my eye I see that he's smirking as he looks down at me, but I can't bring myself to face him fully. Every time I do, I think that I kissed those lips. I seduced him. Ate up. Those *amazing* lips. And that wasn't all. I've told him so many things about me. I always marvel at how easily this man makes me verbally vomit all over him.

"I got the Alcore updates. Good job."

Oh god.

I don't know what to do. I miss my family. I want my grandma's advice. I can't talk to my brother about this. Farrah and Veronica would say I should enjoy yielding to my infatuation of him, the first of my life. They wouldn't understand that a part of me fears I'll want more. The homesickness I've been battling threatens to reappear.

My floor comes up, and I glance at him with a smile and say, "Have a good day, Mr. Carmichael."

His lips shape a thin smile that echoes his tone of voice. "Callan," he corrects me.

"I'll only call you Callan when we're alone. Otherwise, it's Mr. Carmichael."

"Lucky for you, I respond to both." He reaches out to hold the door as I step out. "Are you still up for sightseeing?"

"Always," I blurt without thinking. It's the second time he's asked, and the second time I blurt out the same answer without thinking better of it.

How does he *do* that?

My toes are curling under his stare. "Where are you planning to go?" he asks.

"Navy Pier. I went there with Wynn but I'd love to go again."

Lights of mischief spark up in his eyes. "You must really love that Ferris wheel."

"Oh, of course," I laugh.

He leans closer. "I'll take you to the Pier tomorrow."

"What? I don't think it's a good idea. I really think—"

"Pick you up at five." He presses the button to shut the doors and as they do, he raises his brows in challenge, and the doors shut.

PIER

He's downstairs, behind the wheel of his black-on-black Range Rover. I hurry to the car even as he steps out to open the passenger door.

I greet him with a nervous, "I brought a hat."

He takes his seat behind the wheel and shuts the door behind him. "Preventing freckles?" One brow goes up, along with the corners of his lips.

"Clusters of freckles on my face, yes."

I slide the cap over my head, and Callan reaches out and tucks a strand of hair behind my ear that had ended up flat over my eye.

The touch flits across my skin and down my entire body, making me shiver.

He smiles, *noticing* my shiver.

I gulp and lift my hand, fingering and readjusting my Dallas Cowboys cap in nervousness.

We start driving and I watch his hands on the wheel as he steers. I try to look away because I've been brainwashing myself that this is only a friendly outing. Having Callan catch me staring at his hands like some ogling, adoring idiot won't do.

"Are you up for some excitement?" he asks me.

"Speed and altitude? Are you trying to get rid of me?" I mock frown.

"Nah. I might miss the excitement of anything outrageous you want to share. I'm selfish like that."

"Oh, so you won't murder me because I'm entertaining to you."

He smiles and parks his car, and we head toward the long, bustling corridor of Navy Pier. I point to the colorful horse carousel. "I'd go on that."

"Go to Disneyworld. Better fit for you." He lifts my cap, rumples my hair, and laughs as he sets it back down. I'm smiling as I fix my hair and we head down the corridor and I take in the scenery of restaurants, shops, and entertainment stands, and the imposing Ferris wheel in the distance.

"Now I feel like I'm in Chicago." I stick my tongue out at him.

"Ah. You thought you were in Texas all this time."

"No, I thought I was dreaming." I laugh. "I wasn't very smart, grade-wise. I always had to put in double the effort than others in my class."

"Most of the time, effort trumps talent."

"True." I nod, my lips curving. "So you built Carma on your own?"

He nods.

"I can't believe what you've accomplished on your own, you're still too young." We take a seat on a bench, and I glance around the Pier. "That's what I plan to do the next couple of years. Work. I've never been so exhausted in my life, though. It's like my whole life has been taken over by you and Carma."

He laughs softly, and takes my cap and turns it around.

"No!" I laugh. "I'll get freckles this way."

"That's the plan."

I scowl and notice the heat in his eyes, blushing as I quickly straighten the brim.

"Are you like this with all the women you know?" I narrow my eyes.

"Like what?"

"I'm not going to say it."

"Come on, say it," he dares, shifting in his seat to stretch his arm out behind me.

"Only because we're out of the office and you're wearing a polo and you look like you."

"I *am* me."

"You look a little untouchable in a suit. You don't invite conversation when you look all stuck up and harsh." I inhale. "This *attractive*. All week, Janine apparently answers calls from your girls. 'Is Callan in? Please tell him x, y, and z called.' They're all hopelessly in love with you."

"I assure you, they're not. Many are friends. Others, acquaintances—no strings."

I nearly snort.

He crosses his arms, eyeing me in speculation. "Think I should call them back?"

I start at that, mute.

"Olivia."

I lift my head. His eyes are studying me intently as one sleek eyebrow goes up. "Think I should call them back?"

"I suppose if you want to."

"So you're telling me I should do exactly as I want."

"I mean if you want to talk to them." I'm so jealous I feel literally green.

"Let's see." He pulls out his cell phone and dials.

I inhale painfully—when suddenly, my phone buzzes and NOT DRAKE appears on the screen.

I'm puzzled but pick up, scowling at him. "What are you doing, Drake?"

"Not Drake." He disconnects the call with a press of his finger, looking at me.

"Not the mail guy either," I whisper.

"That's right." He takes my chin and turns my face to his, forcing me to look into his beautiful copper eyes, which seem to see right through me. "Just me."

I turn my head a little bit and busily tuck my phone away. Nervous.

Callan just stands and shoves his hands into his pockets and watches me with this smile on his face. "Olivia."

"Hmm?"

"There's a giant cluster of freckles on your face."

"Shut up!" I groan, laughing because I'm blushing.

We walk down the pier in silence.

I want to kiss him and hold his hand; I want to do many things. I'm surprised by how much I *want* them.

"I sometimes worry I'll end my life doing nothing that I wanted to do," I say as we keep walking along the corridor.

He steals a look at me that clearly says, "Oh, are we talking personal again?" And it's an amused look, so I just grin and fall quiet for a moment.

"So what do you want to do?" he asks me.

"Be my own boss one day. Travel," I admit. "I want to help businesses, but I worry about choosing the ones I could most make a difference for. I'll be no use to anyone if I run my own business into the ground." I shoot him a soft smile. "I want to enjoy my grandma, too, you know. I mean, I know I don't have her forever. I want to enjoy my parents and form a family like they have, but that needs a partner, and sometimes it feels like things going the way you hope isn't even in you or your partner's hands . . . it's sometimes not meant to be."

His eyebrows pull together into a frown. "I wholly disagree. I don't leave things to chance. You want it, you make it happen; if not, you won't."

"That's not true. So many people want things they strive for their whole lives and they're always elusive; other people don't want things that they take for granted. Like my family, for example. Living with them, I felt safe all my life, all my problems solved, yet it still felt like my life was a series of little dramas, from the slight of a friend to Daniel Radisson not wanting to hire me, and the tree house, and me saying the wrong things. I always had their love but I forgot the little dramas. Being away from them I've realized how much I depend on them to feel safe. Even my fear of heights. Or the one where I'll die young and never be anyone's wife or mother. I console myself I'd at least be buried with my parents."

"I don't go thinking about my fears—hell, I don't base my decisions on them." He gives me a wink. "So the saying goes, there are two dogs barking over your shoulder, fear or determination. Which one wins? The one you feed. Never feed the dog who's afraid."

"But you're feeding the dog that tells you relationships don't last. That dog will always win until you stop feeding it."

"Then I won't. I'll feed that dog plump and well."

"You're so stubborn, I pity the girls who fall even half in love with you."

"Yourself included?"

I roll my eyes. "Oh definitely. I'm just pitying myself so hard right now because I will for sure die alone. Nobody's wife and mother."

"But very well made love to every night."

I feel this awful blush run all over me.

What do you want from me?

"My friend Lisa," I tell him. "She's a girl I knew . . . well, she was like a sister for the brief time I knew her. She was Tahoe's first girlfriend." I feel pain when I remember the hurt my brother went through. "She died before she could even legally drink. It caused such an impact. I remember how pale she was in the end, and how weak, and how sad I was to imagine her not being able to live her life longer and experience more things. No matter how much her loved ones tried to bring happiness into those bleak white hospital walls, it was just . . . not meant to be. You can't say that was her choice."

"I'm not going to." His expression softens. "I'm sorry."

"Thanks." I watch our feet and then stop walking and turn to face him. "Tell me one fear of yours. One, Callan. Or I'll never, ever talk to you again. You're freaking inhuman."

He laughs. "I'm so human. You have no idea."

"Prove it."

He scowls, but then we start walking again, and he says, "Being trapped."

"You mean physically?"

"In any way, shape, or form. By the very things I want to have."

"Hmm," I say thoughtfully, the wheels spinning in my mind. "So is that why you can't commit to one company? You just take what you want and drop it so you're free to move on with no commitment or emotional investment in making it work. Takeovers."

"Miss Roth," he scoffs, tugging my ponytail, "I do *nothing* out of fear. I do it because I'm good at it. Because I can. Let's not forget I'm the best at it."

"Any person in the world can give a life or take it; it doesn't mean you should."

"All right then. Because it's all I know. I don't know how to do it differently." His lips curl as he raises one inquiring eyebrow. "My brother and his roughhousing, remember?"

"Yeah."

"Well, five years older is a lot when you're five. I had to devise plans to get what he had and win the game without physically wrestling it from him."

"It was your mode of survival. I'd like to meet this evil brother."

"He's not evil, he's just a sibling; we were both fighting to be the alpha of the house."

"Well, who won?"

"We're still fighting it out."

"Ha ha. I want to meet him, then."

"I don't want him to meet you."

I flush at the possessiveness in his eyes. God. The way he pays attention makes me so self-conscious and aware of him.

"So he's a bad boy, huh?"

"More like you could fire up holy water."

We sit on a bench and sip on cold drinks. His words, though they make me giggle, tug at all of my heartstrings, and every inch of my sexy parts too.

"You have a way of opening me up," I accuse.

He shifts forward on his elbows, glancing at me past his shoulder. "You have a way with me, period."

"I'm not sure we should flirt; it's not professional."

"I agree, it's not." He nods somberly, his hazel eyes watching me.

"Well then, no flirting."

"Miss that pink on your cheeks? I don't think so. I'll have some of that pink with an extra spoonful on the side, Miss Roth."

"You're a cad."

"You like me best when I'm a cad."

"I do not."

"I can say anything right now, bring on the pink, and you will have a very hard time proving me wrong."

"I pity the girls who fall for that. Losers, all of them. I'm not falling for that or you."

"I'm not asking you to."

"What are you asking for?"

"Just time with you." He gazes deeply into my eyes, and slowly, Callan lifts his brows at me.

I stare at the laces of my sneakers. I'm not sure he's making a pass at me. I'm not sure of my own name.

He gets a phone call.

"Carmichael," he answers. He motions with his head for us to leave, and I toss my empty water bottle into a nearby trash can and follow him to the Range Rover.

Several hours after Callan drops me off, he texts me at 9 p.m., making me cancel an evening plan with Wynn. He wants me at his home office. Lincoln is also there with a thousand printed pages of Callan's new obsession. I'm kind of relieved Alcore is off the hook, and in a way, so am I, for having proposed it as ripe for takeover—for now.

At 11 p.m. Lincoln excuses himself to go home and recharge, leaving Callan and me poring over company documents.

By 1 a.m., I'm ready to bail.

"Come on, stay," he says. He sounds almost disappointed that I'm giving up already.

"So I get a peek at a strumpet in the morning? No thanks."

"No strumpets," he says.

I shoot him an I-don't-believe-that look but I stay and even make some coffee for us.

At 3 a.m., I set down the papers and doze off to him speaking on the phone with someone overseas.

I feel a delicious warmth spread over me and hands shift me on the couch—then I sense something hard beneath my cheek and a hand stroking the back of my head. I turn a bit and realize my head is on his lap, his hand running down my hair, stroking me.

Sunday morning I wake up to the sound of male voices. I'm disoriented, glancing around and trying to adjust my eyes to the blazing sunlight pouring through the massive arched windows before me.

Someone covered me with a blanket and plumped a pillow under my head.

It takes me a second to realize where I am and another to realize I must look a sight. Attempting to reach the stairs that lead to the second landing, where I assume both the master and guest bedrooms are located, I pass the conference room downstairs and hear a group of men talking animatedly. They're talking in legal terms and I realize they're Carma's law team.

Seven men sit at the conference table, while Callan is the only one standing, wearing the same shirt he wore last night, his jaw shadowed from a day's growth of beard, his chin resting on two fingers as he looks down at the team with a stance that says "NO BULLSHIT."

I would have never, ever in my life expected my mailman to live in a place like this. To be like this. I can't believe that once, ages ago, I imagined he had a one-bedroom apartment, very cluttered—not a Gold Coast home, with a gated entrance, so clean that the floor could be a long, endless marble mirror beneath me.

His energy fills the room. I can see the men scramble to please him and answer his questions. Tall and dark and solemn, he looks about as brooding and bloodthirsty as a vampire acquiring his next ounce of blood. In this case, a struggling business.

Rolling his shirtsleeves to his elbows while he speaks on the phone, he seems oblivious to the men in the room, even to my presence at the door as I wonder if I should say hello or simply go freshen up and leave.

I see the way he frustratedly tugs the top button of his shirt and I wonder if I hallucinated the way he ran his fingers through my hair last night. His hands are tanned, and although big, they are sleek, his fingers long and elegant. His hair is close-cropped, ending just where his collar begins.

I wonder who the guy on the other end of the line is, probably some other investment-savvy genius like him, and for a moment I'd do anything to listen in on their conversation.

Ending the call with a brusque click, Callan finally turns, assesses his employees in one sweeping motion and, to my mortification, suddenly spots me by the door with my hair probably a mess and in the same clothes as yesterday. He lifts a brow and drinks me in.

And I quickly turn away and hurry upstairs, my cheeks red. I head into a guest bathroom and wash my face and find some toothpaste and mouthwash, then I fix my hair and clothes, call a cab for myself, and tiptoe inconspicuously out of the house.

AT THE GALLERY

Wynn invited me over to her gallery on Wednesday afternoon, and I'm helping her set up her new artist's exhibition. My job is the first thing she asks me about, and I'm nervously selecting what to say about it. "It's consuming," I settle on.

"He was asking me questions about you the other day," she admits.

"What do you mean?" I stand in the middle of the gallery space, surrounded by one wall hung with canvases, the other empty.

"Just if you had a guy back home," Wynn says as she lifts one of the works that will go up on the empty wall.

My eyes widen. "Are you serious?"

"Yeah, that's what I thought. He's not like that. I mean, he's been playing the field for years." She *tsk*s and shakes her head. "I smell sex, Livvy. And lots of it."

"No!" I cry. "I mean . . ." I can't tell Wynn, even though I want to. "He was the first real friend I found in this city, and though it's complicated now, I feel . . . a bit of a weak spot for him, in a way I can't explain."

"I'm thinking he has a weak spot for *you*," Wynn says. She smiles at me tenderly, then hoists a small oil on canvas up on the wall. "Tahoe would go ballistic, Livvy."

"I know! I know. Which is why I'm trying to keep it professional."

"I'm not sure I'd want to be you right now. These boys can be so irresistible."

I glance at Wynn helplessly, not knowing what to say.

"Get your fix from some other guy. Or get a toy," Wynn says.

LATE NIGHTS

've had time for neither. I've hardly found time for anything other than work. Even time to *sleep*. He's been calling in the middle of the night.

"What do you think of HITT on the NASDAQ?"

"Huh?"

"What do you think of High Intelligence Tech Transfor-
mation?"

"It's 3 a.m."

"You know what they say when you wake up at 3 a.m.
Someone's watching you."

"Very funny. Asshole. Now I'm scared."

"Good. Open your computer, tell me what you think . . ."

"Why?"

"Because I told you I'd teach you—you don't get to pick
the times when you want to learn. Now I'm waiting, Livvy."

Between the late-night phone calls, his current takeover and his increasing interest in Alcore, and Mr. Lincoln getting hit with a stomach bug, I'm consumed by his demands for the week and am amazed how he accomplishes all that he does.

I don't even know how the guy fits partying into his schedule, he seems like he's always in one place with a hand in another.

Callan is at a polo match on Friday afternoon when I need to deliver some printouts he requested to review over the weekend.

I arrive during the middle of the match and take a seat at one of the back tables, occupying myself by skimming over the papers to keep from drooling over my boss. He rides a black horse named Kaz, and when the match ends, I follow him to the stables. He hops off and leads his stallion into the stall, wearing riding boots and tight pants that put the sexy butts of baseball men to shame.

"I miss Sara," I say as he pats his horse's neck.

He unbuckles the saddle, admiring the animal's movement. I'm from the South. I appreciate a guy who can take care of horses and ride them the way this guy does. He raises his brow. "Sara?"

I add, "My pinto mare."

"This is Tinkerbell." He signals to a lovely white mare in the stall next to Kaz's.

"Can we ride them?"

We end up riding them in one of the pens, and I wear out poor Tinkerbell as Callan and Kaz chase us around. I remember riding Sara over the meadow in the back of my home, and how free I felt. That same freedom rushes in my veins as I thunder with the mare beneath me, Kaz's hooves thundering behind me, and a guy I'm only too aware of chasing after me.

I feel oddly aroused and breathless by the time we dismount, feed the horses, and head to the Range Rover in the parking lot. He drives me home before he goes change for a business dinner.

I meet him at his house Saturday morning like he asked, and I expect to find some strumpet strutting half-naked around somewhere. I'm surprised that there isn't. Only his naked body on the bed, covered by a sheet.

For a moment I stand by his bedroom door, not knowing what to do, but the AC is at full blast and for some reason I feel the urge to go and pull the sheet a little higher.

He rolls over, stirring awake. I slowly step back, flushing over being caught.

"I was supposed to make sure you got this today." I set the folder on the nightstand.

He shifts up on one arm, his muscles flexing with the move, and he stares at me.

"And I actually also brought coffee," I add, flushing harder.

He squints and takes the coffee cup. "Thanks." His voice is gruff with sleep still. I wonder if he was with anyone after the business dinner and almost want to retch at the thought.

"Callan, you really need to give me more than this," I say, thinking if I'm to be suffering through the wicked temptation of seeing him half naked, it should at least be worth it. "I want to be in on the action!"

He lifts his brows at my brazenness, then chuckles. "You wouldn't know what to do with action if it stared you in the face."

"Yes, I would."

"So, I'm a struggling cellular phone company, my assets are my customer base, which is slowly trickling away and heading to the competition. What are you gonna do?"

"Well, that's easy. I would come up with a new model phone they have no choice but to buy."

"The banks don't loan to you anymore, you're up to your gills in debt."

"Oh. Hmm . . . See, that's why I want to learn! I want to learn from the best. Not only with hopeful eyes of making a company work, but with realistic ones that would help me spot a sick horse from a dead horse."

He chuckles heartily—his laugh making me blush for some reason—and he drags a hand over his jaw then flings the sheets off him and stands to get dressed.

Giving me a very real, very jaw-dropping view of his ass.

He gives me a ride to the office, and I'm still reeling a little bit from the sight of his perfect bare butt.

"If I'm going to be spending this much time with you, you should at least give me some good, solid business tips. Real ones," I complain, still brooding over his gorgeous, unattainable butt.

"All right then." He eyes me, lifting a brow in challenge. "It starts with the way you dress. You can dress easy on any day but important days. You need to mean business, and you need to look the part."

"A.k.a. the dress code? Help your staff get into the business mentality?"

"We're not dicking around here. What we do is serious."

"Okay, okay," I say, because he sounds so passionate about it.

"Those who follow the crowd usually get lost in it." He shoots me a meaningful look. "Don't talk, act. Don't say, show. Don't promise, prove." He slices an invisible path in the air with his hand. "Your actions and your words should always be in line." He looks at me cuttingly. "Tell me I can't, then watch me work ten times as hard to prove you wrong."

It's the unapologetic conviction in his words that get me hard. Like a punch in the balls, making me want to take action.

"When you've got your sights on something, don't look at it independently. It's not what the company is worth on its own, but what it's worth to us at Carma. EXR as an online advertising company loses money, has no way to capitalize on its users, but if we took their user database and added it to our own paying customer base at Carma, and in turn offered our advertisers more reach as we expand their advertising using the EXR vendor sites, the company value grows exponentially for us.

"EXR doesn't want to be bought out, but when you're struggling, you usually have no choice. EXR traded a percentage of its stock with a smaller company in their efforts to stay afloat. Take over and you are closer to having a controlling interest of them both. As they see us approach, they'll try to find another buyer, one who will accept their terms rather than ours. Our job is to not let that happen. Corner them, so to speak."

"See, but you could also form an alliance, share Carma shares with them—"

"No one gets a piece of Carma."

"Okay then, supposing you trade them just a bit of your business savvy in exchange for controlling interest."

"That's what we do. They can stay in their own company, I'm just steering them off the rocky path."

"Not always, sometimes you make them disappear."

"Sometimes, yes."

My face crumples at that.

"I'm not an asshole, Olivia. I'm just the only one who says what everyone else is thinking—who has the balls to do what everyone else is afraid of doing."

I nod, then stare out the window and process it all. "You're like this with women too, aren't you?" I suddenly ask.

I meet his gaze.

He clenches his jaw and stares out at the road as we approach downtown. "Maybe I am like that."

"Do you bring them home?"

"No. Hotels, my Miami house, the apartment in Cabo, or my London flat."

"Just to avoid bringing them home?"

"I compartmentalize. I'm a genius mastermind in that regard. Though sometimes it's hard to follow my own rules."

"Because they're silly," I tease. "Also I think you don't bring them there because you can be terribly selfish and extremely territorial over your space."

He smirks, his eyes dancing with amusement. "Yeah. It has to be that."

"Yet, *I'm* not going anywhere. At least for a little while. I mean, professionally," I hastily amend.

He eyes my lips for a second, then looks into my eyes. "Yeah." Then he glances away, smiling secretively to himself.

I inhale and wonder if I have the courage to tell him that I like him, so much that I couldn't admit I was jealous just now, that I don't know how frustrating it will be to see him kiss and take all these women, one after the other, everyone except untouchable me.

He glances my way, and laughs as if I press his buttons a little too much for his liking. Then he shakes his head—as if denying the chemistry between us, because that's how it needs to be for me—and he pulls out the thick volumes on VIKTOR from the backseat of his car.

I start reading, my brain working like a sponge as I listen to the passionate way he explains the good aspects about the company, the bad, and what he'll do with it when he gets his hands on it.

I'd seen him as someone who broke things apart, but at the end of the evening, I can't help but realize he's a fixer. He likes fixing things that aren't working as much as I like learning this new tidbit about him.

BOARD

I follow Mr. Lincoln into the conference room on Wednesday, where the twelve board members of Carma Inc. are seated at a long, modern mahogany table.

Callan turns to look directly at me.

He casts an approving glance at the red bra strap peeking from under my shirt.

We exchange a subtle look of amusement.

What can I say? I haven't had time to do laundry this week.

For a long moment I look back at him, studying his face without hurry, feature by feature. His eyes drink me up too.

I sit behind Mr. Lincoln as they begin to discuss Alcore— and my heart skips when I'm asked about the company details, which I know by memory now.

It's a brief meeting, really. Mr. Lincoln remains speaking with a few of the board members when Callan walks outside and into a room next door, motioning me inside.

I follow him, shutting the door behind me.

As he watches me walk forward, his eyes snag on the red bra strap peeking out from under my silk button shirt.

"Not in the dress code, I know." My eyebrows lift daringly. "Are you going to take it off too?" I dare, referring to my bandana.

"Sit over here."

He pats the desk to his right.

Heart pounding, I swallow a lump of desire in my throat.

Taunting a jaguar is probably not a good idea, is it?

I sit on the desk.

"Do you want me to take it off?" he asks, sliding a hand to my hip.

"Yes." I swallow.

He brushes my hair back. Clutches my face. Leans toward my ear. "You taunt me." He brushes his lips to mine—the merest brush, a punishment maybe, but a shock runs through me and I lean forward and part my lips.

He tugs my shirt free from the waistband of my skirt. He eases his hand underneath, his fingers warm as he unhooks the front clasp of my bra.

"Shrug it off," he whispers, rough, in my ear.

"Don't," I breathlessly begin, slipping my arms under my shirt to do as he asks, "taunt *me*." I smile, stand up, and drop my bra in the middle of the floor and sashay out of the room to absolute, electric silence.

I'm grinning when I'm back in my office chair, but when my braless breasts bounce beneath the fabric of my shirt, I groan.

God, I'm such a slut for him. Why did I do that? And why did he not take me somewhere private so he could take off the rest? He's the most fucking difficult-to-seduce womanizer I've ever met in my life. He doesn't take advantage of my one crazy moment of weakness.

Fuck
My
Luck!

HIS HOME, AFTER ALCORE

We're in his home that night, beneath the warm yellow lights, where he can skim some of the reports he asked Mr. Lincoln for after the board meeting.

"So the Alcore takeover is happening," I say.

Neither of us is talking about the bra incident.

Thank goodness.

I can't believe I did that.

A little crazy moment of flirting that won't happen again (I've already stashed all my red things away to be *sure* of it).

Wow. I've turned into a Carmichael groupie. My brother would be *so* proud.

Callan keeps skimming the pages, his face etched in concentration as he absently says, "I'm interested." He licks his thumb and flips to the next page.

"What do you mean you're interested? You're going after it!"

He lifts his head and meets my gaze, then shuts the folder and tosses it aside, shifting on the couch to face me. "I intend to, but not until certain factors come into play. Alcore needs to be absolutely helpless."

"Wow. You're an asshole."

"A very rich asshole, Miss Roth." His lips tilt even as I frown. "You can't do business in here, Olivia," he taps a fist to his chest, "you need to use this," then taps a finger to his temple, "and this." He taps his fist to his stomach, the movement pressing his shirt against what I know are perfectly cut abs. "Your gut."

He watches me like he usually does when he expects me to bombard him with questions, but when I don't, he adds, "Alcore's net income doesn't reflect the true state of their company, the cash flow is terrible and the market they're in is a competitive environment. But . . ."

"But?"

"We've got the infrastructure to turn that around. My brother is a gambler and in a way so am I, except I don't leave anything to chance. Which is why I'm dotting all the *i*'s and crossing all the *t*'s first."

I stare thoughtfully at the closed folder on the coffee table. "There's always the chance of failure."

"Failure is not an option." He props his elbows on his knees and shifts forward an inch in my direction. "Only delays. Besides, regrets are for pussies. Shit happens. You deal with it and push forward. End of story."

He lifts his brows, and I nod.

God, this man is cold-blooded.

"You need to always be hungry for more. Win or lose," he adds.

I know that he thinks I'm too sentimental to be in this line of business. He always frowns when I get concerned about somebody getting hurt in the process of a takeover.

Somebody always gets hurt, Olivia; the point is to make a clean cut and grow from there.

I clutch my stomach as I think about Alcore soon being Carma's next target. "I'm nervous now." I frown. "I feel guilty for bringing Alcore to your attention."

"It's your job."

"It's harder than I thought."

He stretches out an arm behind the couch, eyeing me with a serene strength and peace—with no doubt about what he does, or who he is.

"I'm scared of this business being too much for me," I admit.

He reaches out and pushes a stray lock of hair behind my forehead, the touch so unexpected, I tense all over—from my temple to my throat, my chest, my tummy, my thighs, my toes.

"Hey, you're doing good." He nods, and suddenly his eyes grow warmer than usual, almost tender. "Sitting here, I see a girl with more gumption than I've seen in a long time. She's sensitive. Smart. With a pretty good head on her shoulders, who won't take my crap. She's got a nice heart, not very common in Carma. She's young and has a lot to learn. But she's no coward." He shakes his head sternly. "All she needs is a chance to see she's more than one tiny, insignificant fear, and the world is hers."

"You need glasses. Should I tell your temp to schedule an appointment? A doctor, too? Check your head maybe? You're not as smart as they say you are."

He laughs.

I feel my cheeks warm and a strange shyness flit through me. "Thank you," I finally say.

"That'll be six hundred an hour." He opens his palm—his very big palm.

"Wow, really? A shopping spree does just as much good for me and at least I get to keep the shoes!"

He laughs, and when a silence falls, I know it's time to go.

I swallow and I stand quietly and start gathering my things, slipping my feet into my shoes, aware of Callan watching me. He picks up the files again—and it almost feels as if we're both trying very hard to pretend we don't enjoy our conversations so much. As if we're both trying to pretend we don't enjoy sex together too much.

"Well . . . good night, Mr. Carmichael."

For a moment, Callan just stares at me. I almost think he's going to ask me to stay—and not to review papers. But then he says, quietly, "Good night, Miss Roth."

SUMMON TO THE TOP

The rest of the week flies by in a flurry of activity as Mr. Lincoln meets with Callan upstairs on Friday. He heads up the elevator at 9 a.m. with a stack of thick files and paperwork, comes back down an hour and a half later, absently asks me for coffee, copies, more research, corrections, and hours later, he's heading back to meet the boss.

I wonder what they talk about. I wonder what's happening. I'm a cat like that, too curious for my own good, but I can't help it.

I stay late that day, even after Mr. Lincoln leaves, busy organizing the files he's been updating. I'm engrossed in all the details as I type the corrections on the computer, when the phone rings and I absently lift the receiver and recite the usual greeting. "Carma Inc. Henry Lincoln's office."

"Livvy."

I start when I recognize the male voice on the other end of the line.

It's puzzling, really, that a mere voice can affect me this much.

What does he want? I ask myself as I nod stupidly with the telephone clutched tightly in my hand.

"I bumped into Lincoln on his way down. I wanted to see if you were still in."

I swallow. "I am."

He makes a noncommittal sound like "hmm" or "huh," then hangs up.

I'm busy typing again when the back of my neck prickles pleasurably.

I glance up from my computer to spot Callan heading over to me. I'm having trouble finding my voice. "Hi," I say.

He leans over my desk, an intent look in his eyes. "I'm going to have a cigarette upstairs. Do you want one?"

"I've got so much to do—"

He levels his gaze with mine and phrases it differently. "Come upstairs with me, Olivia."

There's something a little hot in his eyes, and very bossy.

I swallow and lock up my drawers, powering off my computer, my heart pounding as I follow him.

We take the elevators upstairs.

Is it wrong? That I'm waiting for him to make a move? This is scandalous. This little secret thing between us. A little bit dangerous. I *know* it's a little bit dangerous. I don't know what it is that we've started, but I'm waiting for it.

My temperature is rising.

I'm silent—expectant—as we head outside to the terrace and settle on one of the lounges.

"I didn't sleep much last night."

"I slept like a baby," I lie.

He laughs in disbelief.

The space between us, it's too large.

He drags a hand over his face, then drops it as he looks at me. "I want more of you, Livvy." His eyebrows are low over his eyes, telling me he's just as frustrated. "I'm trying to do the right thing, but I'm not a good guy."

"Yes you are."

He seems both amused and surprised by my emphatic tone, warning me, "I'm the guy who leaves before you wake up and never says goodbye."

"Well, because goodbyes are terrible," I admit, then when he says nothing, I add, "You're a pretty decent guy. I've wanted to know you since I first saw you. I wondered and wondered. But after what's happened between us, it seems less like a good idea and more like trouble."

"Fuck trouble. Jesus. Just fucking go out with me, Livvy." He studies my features.

I don't even know what to reply, I'm simply digesting what he said while my stomach turns hot.

He eyes me in silence. "The night you woke up in my place after falling asleep on my couch . . . you looked stunning," he says.

"Oh god, don't even mention it. I woke up with my hair all crazy and just . . . No. I can't even think it. And then you won't even let me strut my good stuff, with this demure little uniform."

He shakes his head, his eyes shining. "Livvy, you're fascinating to look at. Even in the same clothes everyone else is wearing."

"Is that why you asked me out, because you like how I look?" The girly part of me, the vain part, wants that to be the reason, but the girl who went to college and studied every weekend wants his attraction to be based on more than that.

"No." He smiles in amusement as if he can read my mind.

I remember when I met him, the very first day, my Hot Smoker Guy.

What would I do if he were still just that guy? Removed of any preconceived notions of whether he could be someone I am allowed to openly like.

His features are completely unreadable as he looks at me, pulling out his pack of cigarettes and lighting one up. Soon, he's taking a slow, very long hit from his cigarette, and then releasing a slow exhale, his lips pushing the smoke out in the sexiest way imaginable.

Damn him. He looks so gorgeous. I don't want to look at his hands, but I do, and they are big . . . big and manly.

I remember our sex positions when we had those amazing nights.

He hands me the cigarette as he exhales, and I take a hit. "I want us to see each other out of the office. Monogamously."

I inhale so much smoke I start coughing, my eyes wide.

"Have you been seeing anyone else?" He frowns darkly and lightly pats my back to help me recover.

"No."

"Do you want to?" he asks, raising a brow.

"No."

"Neither do I. That's the problem."

"Why is that a problem?"

"Well, Olivia. I'm staring at a woman who's got me in the throes of lust twenty-four/seven almost—and I've got work to do. Physically, I've never felt this deprived. Keeping my hands off you is testing my willpower to an extent beyond my limits." He slips his hand on my thigh, squeezing it. "I want you nightly."

"Haha. Really."

"Really." He touches my face. "I want you. Again. And again and again."

"I want you too. Except let's not forget I'm leaving."

"I know full well you're leaving," he takes a drag, frowns, exhales and passes the cigarette to me, "that you're T's sister, that you work for me. I'm also fully aware that we can't keep our hands off each other. That you distract the shit out of me. That you're irresistible on every level. And that I don't want you to see anyone else, period."

"Even if I wanted to, I'm too busy working. You're a slave-driver. No offense."

"None taken." He grins.

I look at his profile and want to kiss him but I'm also unsure if I've got the skills to really engage in an affair, go back to Texas, and come out unscathed. "I don't want to miss out on learning things because we're in the bedroom."

He laughs. "We can do both." He lifts my chin. "I've got a mind to spend insane amounts of time with you, in bed and out of it. If you're up for the challenge. And never fear; Carma time will be absolute business."

"Can I think about it?"

He glances at his watch. "Fifteen seconds."

"Oh, come on! Give me a week."

"You leave in what? Four weeks? That'll take a week off my time." He strokes his hand over my leg again. His pupils are dilated as he watches me smoke, as if he enjoys watching me do something naughty.

"It's not your time. Not *yet*. Wow, I've given you every second of the day this week . . ."

"I want every second of your nights too. I mean to have them."

"Give me one week, Callan," I say. "I'm still high from . . . well, the last time."

He frowns, but leans back on the lounge and spreads out his arm, taking the cigarette I extend, putting it between his lips and drawing a long, deep inhale. He calmly says, his eyes glimmering, "You know you want this as much as I do."

"Maybe." I drop my head to hide the smile on my lips. "Give me until Monday. That's in ten days, not *this* Monday."

"You know your weekdays, good for you, Olivia."

I laugh and nod.

He laughs and pulls me to his chest, and I reach for the box of Marlboros and pull out a second cigarette. Callan takes it and lights it with the last of the first cigarette, then he hands it over and lets me take the first hit.

"I don't sleep with my bosses," I say.

"You mean Lincoln. Thank god."

"Callan." I laugh. "Nope. Just you, it seems."

I offer him the cigarette but he doesn't seem to notice; instead, he stares at my features as he lifts his hand to tuck a loose strand of hair behind my ear so that it won't get in the way of my eyes meeting his. He leaves his thumb on my temple in the smallest caress over my skin and the shell of my ear.

It feels intimate, the way we stare at one another, intimate by saying nothing, just letting him rub his thumb over my ear.

My hands are shaking when I finally extend the cigarette, and he takes it—still watching me.

I watch him.

He inhales as if he has all the time in the world, exhales the smoke out slowly through a slit between his lips, then offers me one last hit, and when I shake my head, he puts it out, neither of us looking away.

God, he looks so handsome right now in black slacks and a wine-colored shirt.

He looks at me with a smile, waiting. Waiting for my answer.

"Let's start with a date. That's all I'm asking to start with."

"You make it sound so simple," I whisper.

"It's simple," he says.

Urgh. Is it?

Why could he not be the mailman like I thought he was? It could be simpler. It could be easier to enjoy a date or two and maybe even hope for a little more if he were the nice, harmless guy I'd thought he was—not my boss, so that everyone can think of me as some office slut; not my brother's friend, so my brother can see me with new disappointed eyes; not some player whose mere attractiveness turns me into one of *those* girls. One of those legions of silly little groupies.

I cannot be one of those, damn it, that'd be so pathetic.

I *am* pathetic! I just caught myself grinning like a fool.

I groan and I hear myself saying, "Okay." I want it to be simple.

He smiles. A brilliant smile. "Pick you up tomorrow then," he says, a quiet statement.

I breathe, nodding. "Tomorrow. But Callan, I don't want anyone to see us—it could get messy and the last thing I need is messy when I've been trying so hard to make a name for myself."

"I understand," is all he says.

I smile and he leans over and places his hand on my waist, pressing his lips to mine, kissing me.

My body—which had been sort of aching for this—kicks into full speed and every part of me starts to buzz as our tongues meet, mesh, play, in the softest, longest, most delicious kiss of my life.

That night, I text Nana on impulse because I need to tell *someone.* My parents will tell me it's not proper. My brother will not be happy I chose him. And my friends wouldn't understand. Nobody would understand except maybe two people in my life, and I can't talk to Callan about it, either.

Nana calls me as soon as she reads my text. I exhale when I hear her Betty White voice, and say a little prayer heavenward that she's free to talk tonight.

So I tell my grandma that I've been sort of seeing/not seeing a guy at work and feel confused.

"Do I get a name for this young man?" she prods.

"He's Callan Carmichael, Nana—"

"Oh my!" Nana says. "My grandson's friend—and your boss?"

"Nana, don't judge."

"I'm not judging."

"Nana, please don't tell Tahoe."

"What biz does this have to do with Tahoe?"

"He's just protective. Callan and he are friends."

"Then he can't be that bad."

"Yes, but he's a notorious womanizer and . . ." I begin listing all the reasons why I shouldn't like him to my nana. "He's really not as adorable as he seems, he's been running me to the ground. He takes over companies that don't want him to take over and squashes them, selling the parts or simply robbing them from the owners to absorb into his other companies and become even richer."

"Smart, ruthless man. How sexy."

"Nana!" I groan. I sigh and add, "I just needed someone to talk to."

"Livvy," Nana says, "you can't have a timeline for when you find the right man for you. The fact that you're focused on work and career doesn't mean that you can't still have time to fall in love."

"But I'm not falling in love," I contest.

"Okay then." She sounds like she doesn't believe me.

"I know I haven't shown real interest in a man before, but it's because you know I have a bigger plan. I was looking at the bigger picture and now he's—" I throw my hands in the air. "Blocking it!"

"Yielding to an infatuation, or whatever you young ones call it these days. Fucking . . ." She snickers. "Is not necessarily a bad thing."

"Oh, Nana!" I laugh hysterically.

"One thing I know for sure," she adds, "is that life has its own timing."

When we hang up, I grab my Queen of Effing Everything pillow and drop on my bed, glancing at my phone and searching NOT DRAKE on the screen.

I grin and lie down, setting my phone aside.

I like how infuriating he is. How he pushes me and brings out my competitive side.

How he smokes and dangles that cigarette from his mouth.

His touch and his kiss.

Hell, I love how he just plain told me he wanted to see me.

I just don't know that I like wanting him like this.

In Nana's generation, she was expected to be just a housewife. When my grandfather passed, she had to raise five kids on her own with no degree, and trust me, feeding five kids on cookie sales and knitting was hard. She always told me how much she would have liked to be prepared to be alone. I want to be more than just a young housewife, though it was nice seeing Rachel and Saint as a family. I definitely picture a family in my future; it's something I've always wanted. Just not now, and I don't think that's what Callan wants either or might *ever* want.

I know he's not asking me for that.

He's just asking for more . . . and I'm afraid if I take that one step, he'll pull me to the ledge and take everything.

I don't like ledges.

But part of maturing is letting go of your fears.

I turn off the light. I think of Callan's gorgeous smile and the sexy movements of his tongue when he kisses me on the mouth and, well, when he kisses me anywhere, really. He's so hot. Addictive. God, he's such a beautiful man, it's not fair to be tempted like this.

I punch my pillow into shape and burrow my cheek in it, trying to get some sleep.

DATE NIGHT

Has anything preceding this moment compared to the excitement I feel for this date?

    You'd think it was my first date. It's *not*.

But my nerves are ridiculous.

It's just the first date with a guy who makes my knees weak and my heart literally throb. Urgh. My Hot Smoker Guy makes my breath slow down until it's nonexistent, or speed up until I'm basically panting for him.

    This is a big no-no, I know. But my body doesn't get it!

    I have spent practically the whole day getting ready for tonight. I went to get my nails done after barely even having breakfast because I was so nervous and excited I didn't feel hungry. I also got a bikini wax. I was tempted to wax it all off, but remembering how Callan seemed to like me natural, I left a nice little landing strip on my you-know-what.

    I then mentally rummaged through my closet for the perfect outfit and decided to go lingerie shopping. Lace, satin, ruffles, sequins, patterns, strings, and bows called out to me from all corners of the boutique lingerie store.

I finally settled on a matching bra and pantie set that I was *sure* would drive Callan crazy. I wanted something sexy but effortlessly so.

When I got home, I tried on the black lace thong that I got with a lovely satin bow on the back, and the black bra with lace detail on the cups. The black makes my skin look smooth and decadent, and I knew I looked good.

Hell, I looked more than good. I got all giddy and danced around my apartment in my new lingerie to sexy music, letting my mind wander to tonight, and how I hoped it would end . . .

Noticing the naughty path my thoughts were taking, I took off the lingerie because I didn't want to ruin it with how, ehm . . . excited I was getting. Already!

I tried to entertain myself the rest of the day until it was time to get ready. I watched some mindless TV and tried to do some things for work, but nothing could get my mind off tonight.

I had woken up that morning with a text from Callan (I figured it was time I changed his name on my contacts), and the way my stomach felt when I saw his name for the first time, really, on my phone screen is indescribable. Butterflies would be an understatement; let's just leave it at that.

I'd been trying hard to keep it just business—but underlying the business there were always these looks.

This *want*.

It's become unbearable.

The text said to be ready by seven thirty, and that he would pick me up at my place.

When the clock struck six, I finally decided to start getting ready. I got in the shower and soaped up until I smelled amazing all over.

I got out of the shower and dry-brushed my skin, and then put on some moisturizer before wrapping myself in my short bathrobe and proceeding to blow-dry my hair.

Ten minutes later, my hair was dry and silky straight. I did my makeup and put on a pair of diamond earrings that my grandma had given me when I turned twenty, and walked into my closet. I decided to wear a red satin dress that flowed around my knees, though the material plastered itself to my breasts and the tops of my thighs whenever I walked. So it was the perfect combination of elegant and sexy. I finished it off with a thin necklace and strappy heels.

The whole time I was getting ready, I kept sneaking glances in the mirror and I was amazed by what I saw looking back at me.

I'm still shocked by what I see as I apply the finishing touches to my lips. I am basically glowing. My eyes are bright, my skin looks smooth, the dress looks like it was made for me, and the smile on my face reflects everything I feel inside.

Which is overwhelming, giddy excitement.

I'm tucking my lipstick and makeup into a small clutch purse when the doorbell rings. My heart trips in my chest as I start for the door. I take a deep breath and turn the knob.

And standing in front of me is the most delectable man on this planet.

Gulp!

Dressed in slim black slacks and a dark gray shirt, the man looks like the deadliest guilty pleasure.

He takes his time drinking me in with a burning warmth in his copper eyes, starting at the tip of my head and traveling to my lips, my breasts, my stomach, and the tips of my freshly painted toes.

I hear him inhale sharply, and the gaze I am met with when he finally meets my eyes steals my next breath.

I see pure, unrestrained lust, and a glimmer of something else. Something possessive. Something feral, something forbidden.

I feel like a switch went off in his head, I feel like his eyes hold a promise in them.

"Olivia," he says. Low.

"Callan."

He smirks, then takes two steps toward me and puts his hands on my waist, pulling me to him and wrapping me up in his intoxicating and delicious smell. He looks down at me and whispers something under his breath.

The next thing I know, he dips his head and places his warm, smooth lips on my neck. He kisses and rubs them across my neck, and I can feel my legs turn to Jell-O. His hand cradles the side of my face as his lips travel to my cheek, where he whispers in my ear, "You look good enough to eat."

"Thank you," I breathe.

"You ready?"

I'm about as ready as can be. I nod. "So we're doing this." I laugh nervously. I duck my head. "Just one date, okay?"

"One date for now." He gently runs his thumb along my lower lip. A rueful smile curves his mouth. "Did you think I only wanted to sleep with you, Livvy?" he asks.

I swallow.

"Was that what you thought I was asking for?"

I'm breathless and flushed, because maybe I did think that.

He moves his hand as if ready to brush my hair back, but instead he peers into my face. "That's not what I want from you. I like you too much. I enjoy being with you." He leans closer and absently tucks a strand of hair behind my ear. "I'm enjoying that shy little pink shade on your cheeks quite a bit right now."

I smile and eye him. "Where are we going?"

"Depends on whether we make it out of here. It's taking every ounce of my willpower not to take you back into your bedroom and bury my head between your legs."

I suck in a sudden startled breath. "Callan!" I lightly smack his shoulder.

He takes the hand that smacked him and looks me in the eye, his stare unapologetic as he kisses my knuckles. He grins. "Come on."

He leads me to the elevator and down to his car.

He drives us in his Range Rover Sport while I silently rational-ize my actions.

Callan seems at ease with what's about to happen, while I sit in a mess of hormones on the front passenger seat.

He drums his fingers as we're stuck at a stoplight for a while. "Fucking traffic," he growls. He lifts his thumb to my face and traces a dent in my cheekbone with his knuckle. "What are you thinking?"

"You know what," I groan.

He smiles. He's not as calm as I think he is, his eyes blazing with hunger. I have never enjoyed a feeling the way I enjoy the way he makes me feel. Grown up, but vulnerable like a little girl. Thrilled but almost scared, as I am when I get too close to the ledge. Warm in all places and like my body got plugged into an electric outlet. My nipples hard, my panties wet.

"I sometimes wonder if I imagined everything that happened the other nights. I'm not sure you're really as good as my memories claim."

"I'm better." He smiles and shoots me an intent stare. "I'm looking forward to tasting you this time, Livvy, sucking that pussy of yours for a long, hard while."

"Oral?"

"That's right. It's driving me crazy not to know what you taste like."

I clutch my thighs together.

Goodness!

I'm *boiling* in my skin.

His Range Rover Sport is all man. Smooth, dark leather and an engine that sounds like a monster ready to be unleashed. It's the kind of car that he tampered with to make fully his—with modifications like a matte finish and a different grille and custom wheels.

People stare as we drive by.

"Don't worry," he says, reading my thoughts, "the windows are tinted."

I gulp and nod, feeling my stomach tie itself up in knots.

"Where are we going?" I ask.

"My place. I'm cooking for you."

My heart rate doubles as I realize we're going to be alone. In his mansion.

Before I finish that thought, he reaches out his hand, palm up, silently asking me to hold it.

Callan Carmichael wants to hold my hand.

I swallow and try to still the throbbing, reckless beat of my heart.

I feel like a teenager again.

I turn to look and see him staring out at the road, his other hand at the top of the wheel, with a cocky smirk on his face. His profile is stunning, with light scruff on his jaw. His hair looks soft and sexy with a slightly messy look, his nose and jaw perfectly defined. His lips smooth and pink, promising a thousand dirty pleasures. His face looks like it was carved by an angel.

He clenches his jaw when I don't immediately take his hand, and then he wiggles his fingers at me and edges his hand closer.

I laugh and he chuckles. I give in and hold his hand.

It's warm and huge compared to mine. His grip is steady and comforting. I let myself relax into the seat, and I'm suddenly met with an overwhelming sense of belonging.

Belonging in this car, next to this man, with my hand in his.

We get to his place, and before I know it we're heading into his home from his huge ten-car garage.

As we cross the living area, I see candles on the dining table and settings for two, with a red rose on the place setting I assume is mine. I smile. "Callan, this is incredible."

I turn to look at him, and he's already looking at me.

He doesn't say anything, just smiles back and kisses me on my forehead.

"You hungry?" he asks, walking to his sprawling kitchen, with an Italian marble island that has plates of cut raw veggies, different-colored peppers, some greens, along with various spices.

"I didn't know you cooked."

He nods, turning on the stove. "Yeah, well. Mother left when we were little. My father tried to make cooking a game for Cullen and me. The kitchen was the one place where we felt like a family."

I'm silent, just listening.

He throws some chopped veggies and potatoes with herbs on the stove and stirs them a little before dribbling some extra virgin olive oil on them. I walk over and peek at the food cooking on the stove. "I hadn't realized I was so hungry until I saw all this," I confess.

He turns around from marinating two steaks on the island and hugs me from behind, places a hand on my growling stomach and lays a kiss on my exposed shoulder. "I got a head start before picking you up. Food's almost ready, baby; you don't have to wait long."

I gulp and try to overlook the fact that he just called me *baby*, but the sound of his deep, rumbling voice calling me his *baby* does some serious things to me. I clench my thighs to-gether, silently begging my body to calm down because we haven't even had dinner yet and I'm already thinking about being in bed.

"So, what did you do today?" I hear Callan ask.

"Oh, nothing, I lounged around the apartment, watched some TV, got my nails done . . ." I trail off and admire him walking around the kitchen, occasionally checking this and that, sprinkling spices and stirring and adjusting temperatures. "What about you?" I ask.

"I went on a run, went to Carma to review some options for our next takeover, bought a painting at an auction. The usual," he responds.

"Sounds like a very busy day."

He turns to look at me, leaning back against the counter with his arms across his chest. "I guess you could call it that. I made an effort to distract myself."

"Why?" I ask.

"Because if I didn't, I would've been at your door as soon as you woke up."

My stomach clenches at the thought, and my heart races.

I smile and answer honestly. "That would've been nice."

We look at each other, a thousand unspoken words fluttering in the space between us, and the moment is broken when the timer for the steaks rings and it's finally time to eat.

We sit down and he pours us both a glass of red wine, the reason being it "enhances the flavors" in the food.

I mock him for that comment but quickly shut up as soon as I take the first bite—because this is seriously some of the most delicious food I have ever tried.

I tell him so, and he just smiles in thank you.

We talk about everything. About Carma, about his anal dress code (I tease him about keeping my bra and hair band somewhere around his house), our favorite foods, my fear of heights, and his reason for smoking. We talk about anything and everything, effortlessly moving from one topic to the next.

I have never felt so comfortable, or so at home, with another human being in my life.

His eyes make me lose track of time. Everything about him drives me crazy . . . his smell, his touch, his voice.

When we're finished eating, we wash the dishes together and finish in no time. At one point, I splash him with water and he solemnly tells me, "Big mistake."

I begin to laugh, but then he picks me up and slings me over his shoulder like a caveman.

I start to shriek and laugh in total delight, all the while demanding he put me down. He walks effortlessly with me slung across his shoulder and lays me down on his couch in front of his huge flat-screen TV.

He places his hands on either side of me, caging me in.

I lean back away from him.

"Playing hard to get?" he demands, staring at me intently but playfully.

I shake my head. "No."

"No?" he repeats, challenging my answer.

I gulp but respond again, "You heard me, Carmichael."

He chuckles, but when I meet his eyes, there's no laughter there. "Kiss me," he says, fluttering his lips over mine.

I don't answer.

"I don't know if you noticed, Olivia, but that was not a question . . ."

My heart speeds up and I feel myself getting wet between my legs as he gets closer to me, his breath fluttering over my lips. I keep trying to act like I don't want to kiss him but I know he can see the truth in my eyes.

I am dying to kiss him. I am dying to taste him. For him to taste *me*.

"Kiss me," he says again, this time more gently.

I look at him, his eyes fiercely looking at mine as his hands frame my face tightly. I see the desire in his eyes, I see the pain, the relentlessness, the ambition; I see caring.

I see a man. A man who I want to love. And a man who I want to love me . . .

I know it's not possible, that I'm too young, and he's too worldly, but in this moment, I sort of tremble with the knowledge that I still want it nonetheless. At least for tonight. For this night.

"Callan . . ." I whisper.

"Kiss me, Olivia," he whispers, huskily now, and with that, I crack, and I raise my lips to his, kissing him with everything I've got, with everything I feel, wrapping my arms around him and pressing my mouth to his, fair and square, tongue and all.

I let all of my confusion, all of my lust, all of my wanting, all of my waiting pour into this kiss. I let it all go. I focus on him, his soft yet firm lips kissing me back just as hard and just as passionately.

He tears his mouth away from mine, only to place it on my neck, and I feel him travel lower, toward my breasts, as though my kiss unleashed his hunger full-on.

I moan.

He brings his mouth back up to mine and we start to kiss again, and we don't stop for what seems like an eternity.

His tongue slips between my lips and it's warm and wet, and it makes me want it someplace else. I moan again and wrap my hands around his neck, welcoming his kiss.

He picks me up and turns us around so he's sitting and I'm straddling him on the couch.

I rub against him, never breaking our kiss. Soft breasts to hard chest.

I feel him hard between my legs and I ache for more.

His hands grip my ass and press me against him, as if he knows I need more.

"God, you're beautiful," he says against my lips.

I kiss him in response, holding on to him, my fingers threaded in his soft hair, pulling his head closer to mine.

He puts his hands underneath my dress and grips my thong-clad ass.

He breaks the kiss and looks at me. "What have we got under here?"

"What . . .? What do you mean 'what'? My underwear."

His hand rubs against my naked ass cheek, challenging what I said.

I roll my eyes at him and he chuckles.

I take his hand and lead it higher, to the bow on the back of my new thong.

He arches an eyebrow. "Let me see it."

His fingers rub the satin of the bow on my ass, and I sit there and let him, looking into his eyes.

"It's not red," I say regretfully, suddenly wishing it were.

"Show me," he says, rubbing his thumb along my bottom lip.

"Show you what?" I whisper, concentrating only on how hard he is between my legs and on his beautiful eyes staring at my mouth.

"Your underwear," he says.

I laugh. "What are you, fifteen?"

He grinds me against him, reminding me that he is most definitely not fifteen, and I gulp.

He plants a kiss on my cheek before leaning back and placing his hands behind his head, apparently waiting for me to dismount him and show him my underwear.

I'm about to ask him if he's serious but the look in his eyes stops me.

He looks like he's about to unwrap the greatest present Santa ever gave him. *Life* ever gave him. He looks like a starved lion about to eat his first meal in days.

He looks like he is about to attack me.

And I am loving every second of it.

And I'm about to make him die for it.

This is why you got the underwear in the first place, Olivia . . . who cares if it's not red? He *doesn't seem to care.*

I try to pump myself up because I'm about to strip for this deliciously sexy man who is basically fucking me with his eyes right about now.

I get off his lap and hear him moan in protest.

I smirk.

I get up and walk so that I'm a couple of feet away from him.

I look him straight in the eye as I start to slowly slip off the straps of my dress.

I see him gulp.

I reach behind me with one hand and slowly draw down the zipper of my dress.

I let the dress fall so that the whole top half of my torso is exposed.

I look down and see my tight stomach, and my full breasts decorated in the black lacy bra.

I run my fingers along the edges of the bra's cups and play with the straps, letting one fall down my shoulder. I look at Callan, and his eyes are fixed on mine. His pupils are so dilated, his eyes almost look black.

I pull down the other strap of my bra and take a step toward him.

"You still haven't shown me what you've got under there . . ." Callan teases. But his eyes are serious.

"Shh, be patient," I say.

I unzip my dress the rest of the way down and let it drop to my feet.

I hear Callan inhale sharply and I see his eyes make their way down my body. I'm left standing in my thong, my bra, and my high heels.

I hear Callan curse under his breath. He stands up and makes his way toward me, but I raise my hand to stop him and take a step back.

I unclasp my bra and let it fall down as well, the cool air that meets me making my nipples pucker, and I see Callan's eyes flare at the sight.

"Do you like what I've got, Callan?" I ask.

He smirks, and takes another step toward me, to which I respond by taking another step back.

"Jesus, Olivia, let me touch you," he growls, and takes another step forward.

I shake my head no, and take another step back, before turning away from him and bending over and taking off my high heels. I unfasten the straps and slip them off my feet, one by one, knowing each second Callan has to wait to touch me will drive him even more crazy. Also knowing Callan is enjoying a very, very nice view of my ass.

When I turn around, I see Callan basically eating me up with his eyes.

"That's it," he roughly whispers.

He wraps me in his arms and kisses the hell out of me. His hands all over my body. He picks me up and wraps my legs around his waist, taking me to his bed.

Finally . . .

We get there and he unbuttons his shirt, tossing it to the ground. He takes off his shoes and socks and unfastens his belt, so he's naked except for his black slacks.

He lays me down and kisses my neck, licking and sucking.

I moan and squirm under him, wanting him to take me already.

His lips find my nipple and he sucks it in his mouth, sending a tingling sensation right between my legs.

He turns his head and takes the other one in his mouth, and I moan in response.

His hand slips between my legs and I feel him tease me through my lace panties. His lips find mine and he kisses me hard and rough, his teeth nipping at my lower lip and his tongue slipping between my lips to taste. His kiss is drugging and delicious, his lips perfectly molded against mine.

His fingers keep working me through my panties and I feel like I'm going to die if he doesn't give me more soon.

"Callan, please," I beg.

He kisses my neck and uses his hand to pull my panties to the side before pushing a finger inside me.

I gasp and hold on to his shoulders, my nails biting into his skin as he slowly pumps his finger in and out.

"God, Olivia . . . you're so tight," he groans as he keeps fingering me.

I whimper and feel myself getting wetter and wetter.

I bite his neck a little. He groans low in his throat, and at the sound, need rips through me. I run my hands over his head, and his hair ends up rumpled and sexy.

I feel drunk, and naughty, and impulsive. I've never been the girl to just go with it, to fuck everything, but this . . . this man . . . this moment . . . this need, I cannot deny myself him. He drags his fingers down my bare abdomen and expertly teases his hand over my panties.

Oh.

God.

My hips jerk in a circle to get closer and I grip the back of his neck for balance.

"You're so responsive. I could tease you all night and get off on watching you." He rubs my sex lightly over my panties and leans over to nibble my lips. He kisses and nibbles my neck and continues to move his finger, making my knees weak when he knowingly passes by my clit.

I've never had this. Even kisses like this. I want to take every feeling apart and figure out its contents and I want to put into words how amazing it feels, and I want to forget about all that and just feel alive, intensely connected, wanted and so, so desirous. I've wanted things, but this wanting is more like an ache or an obsession. I can't seem to pull apart the feeling ei-

ther, or give it a word, so I don't, and just let him finger me,
half dressed at his place, panting and making noises like I'm
some sex kitten.

His toned arms come around me.

He's soon tasting my nipple again with his tongue, long,
warm swipes. He moves his tongue to flick the tip in a circle
around my breast. He squeezes the flesh to push my nipple
deeper into his mouth, and when he has it right where he wants
it, he sucks.

He stops and lifts his head and watches me, lips curled, as
a fingertip circles the sensitized point of my nipple.

He hooks his thumb on the edge of my panties and pulls
them down my legs. Revealing my pussy.

He grabs me by the ass and dips his head downward. "Do
you know what you're getting into?" His eyes are dilated and
swirling with a combination of tenderness, desire, and heat.

His lips press to the inside of my thigh, then trail a delicious path up my abdomen. "Open your mouth and kiss me,"
he says.

I arch my back and stick my tongue into his mouth even
as he plunges his own in mine. He groans as he makes contact.
"You as into this as I am?"

"Mmm . . ."

He ducks his head and a hungry sucking sound leaves him
as he tortures the hardened, sensitized point of my nipple back
in his mouth.

I cling to his shoulders, pleasure cascading through me as
I start humping his hand.

"Callan . . ."

"Callan what?"

"Callan Carmichael—"

"That's right."

He smothers my mouth and kisses me hard again.

We're kissing wetly and heatedly when he withdraws his finger from my tight sheath and continues brushing, grazing. I can't breathe from the anticipation of waiting for him again. I pull my mouth free and press it against his jaw, panting against his skin. Soon I'm holding in my breath, waiting for it—for him to fill me with something, anything at this point would be good.

"Is this what you want?"

He caresses my breast with one hand as he eases the tip of his long, strong middle finger inside me.

I groan out something unintelligible, thrusting my hip out for more.

He pulls it back and smiles.

"You want it or not?" He moves over my slickness and I groan.

"Yes," I gasp.

He pushes it into his mouth and tastes it, and then he pushes it back into my pussy. Already my orgasm is building as he rhythmically starts to finger me.

I undulate to his hand.

He tastes my mouth again, really possessively this time. I'm still not used to feeling this intensity during sex.

Now I get it, why people have heart attacks during sex. Maybe my lungs will just turn to stone because it sure as hell feels like it.

All my energy is gathering in a ball of fire at the core of my body, I don't have the energy to breathe, much less speak. But I somehow manage to breathlessly say, "So . . . *amazing* . . ."

"How much do you want it?" He rubs his thumb over my clit, clenching his jaw as he pushes another finger inside me.

Our eyes meet, and a raw look crosses his features before he lifts his fingers and tastes me, softly, so softly.

"Oh god, that's too hot." I run my fingers over his jaw.

He strokes his hand down my bare thigh. "I really enjoy kissing you. All over," he adds meaningfully.

He looks at my naked body for a whole minute then his hand cups my jaw. His eyes are a mixture of hunger, amusement, and tenderness. He leans over and kisses me, slipping his tongue into my mouth slowly this time, as if I'm irresistible. Meant to be savored.

He eases his hand between my legs to open me wider and parts me so he can taste my pussy.

"Ohhhhh," I hear myself breathe as he licks his tongue slowly along the entrance of me.

His hand clenches my thigh and squeezes, he groans as if he could get off on my taste alone.

I gasp when he dips his tongue inside, deep, deeper . . . deepest. I groan and drag my bare feet up the back of his thighs.

I inhale sharply when he reaches up to massage my breasts, his eyes closed as he tastes me. I watch his face move between my legs and the sight is so hot I'm about to go off.

He starts kissing my sex lips again as he eases his thumb over my clit and starts rubbing in delicious circles. I don't know how to feel, how to react, my world is spinning a thousand miles a minute, there is nothing beneath me, nothing but my arms around his neck, clenching, and his hot mouth, and his expert hands.

I can hear my breathing in the dark, crazy fast, when he withdraws and strips down to his bare sexy bones. And muscles. Lots of muscles and perfection here.

"Who do you want here, Olivia?" he says as he spreads above me, his voice rough in the dark as he straightens.

He takes my hips and parts my legs wider open with a nudge of his knee. He leans over to tease his tongue over the tips of my breasts. I arch in agony and pleasure.

"You, Callan." I'm trembling, gripping him to me.

He grabs his erection and teases the tip inside me. "Say it now." He sounds so possessive, so determined to take it all.

A guttural sound leaves my throat as I lift my hips, desperate for him. "Callan."

He pushes my hips down to pin me in place, then drives forward in one smooth, hard thrust.

"Callan," I groan.

He groans too, laughs and sets his forehead on mine.

"Oh god, Callan," I cry when he teases my clit with his thumb.

He's intent and sober as he thrusts again and thrusts his tongue into my mouth, his body moving sinuously, lithe as a wildcat and muscular as a mustang.

"So right. So goddamned right." He's growling and thrusting now.

"Don't stop," I groan, breasts bouncing from the impact, head rolling to the side.

He catches my hands and places them above my head. He uses his thighs to spread mine farther open as he withdraws. I look at him, and he looks at me.

He drives back in. My eyes flutter shut before he shushes my name and makes me open them. Oh god. I've never loved a man's cock the way I love his. It's hard and thick and long and strong. It's what joins me to him. It's what enables him to take me the way I want to be taken. It's what fills me, right now, with ALL OF HIM.

And I can't get enough.

The muscles of his arms bulge as he laces his fingers through mine. Captive and unable to use my hands, tremors are already racing down my body.

I grip him with my sex, and my mouth, all I can use.

I drag my lips over his jaw, nipping the hard angle.

He looks so hot, I get even wetter, and it feels so good I'm already at the brink.

For a man who has everything, you'd never expect him to be this hungry for one girl. Much less for me.

But Callan is devouring me with his eyes, his hands, and his big, thick cock.

He sucks one nipple, then the other.

He tells me how beautiful I look, how perfect I feel. My body starts tightening in preparation for orgasm, and Callan pulls out, waits one thrilling, anticipatory heartbeat, then holds my arms over my head and plunges back in, deeper and harder.

I convulse as an orgasm rips through me.

"God, you're a wet dream." Callan's gruff, admiring voice filters through as I thrash beneath him.

I want him here with me, and suddenly, with unnatural force, I push him to his back and impale myself down on him. He grips my hips and gnashes his teeth as I ride him. He pumps his hips faster, really fast now. His body jerks and a sound rumbles up his chest.

I hear his delicious groan and I come a little more, feeling his muscles flex and contract. He comes really hard, his cock jerking several times inside me. He rolls us over to the side and continues coming, drawing out the sensation, groaning when he's done.

"Oh god," I moan, clutching him, then laughing happily. "Oh god, that felt so amazing."

He laughs softly in my hair before rolling to his back.

"It's so intense with you. Is it always like this?"

He lifts his brows, his eyes gleaming. "You tell me."

I stare at him, into his gorgeous copper eyes. He lifts his head and licks and suckles my nipples and my smile fades as desire starts up again. I clutch his head as it moves over my breast, the heat of his mouth arrowing to the tenderly aching spot between my legs. "You're very sexy when you do things to me," I admit.

Maybe it was the date or the constant days of sexual frustration that make it intense, I wonder. Or maybe it's just intense. With him. I want to go again.

Well hello, nymphomaniac Livvy!

Hopefully sex maniac Callan won't mind.

He pries free and heads to the giant marble bathroom to clean up, and I curl up on my side and watch the door. He exits the bathroom—all sweaty and naked—and our eyes meet.

I sit up when I notice him lift the sheets with the intention of slipping under the covers with me.

He leans over and takes my lips, leisurely, with no rush. "I really, really enjoy kissing you." The husky murmur is whispered against my mouth.

"Am I sleeping here?" I'm wondering out loud whether I should get dressed to be taken home.

His arm slides possessively around my waist as his chuckle prickles through me.

"Not sure how much sleeping there will be. But I'm not going anywhere. Neither, for that matter, are you."

It's dark. The only sounds those of wet kissing and whispers. Raw and hoarse. I'm straddling him, his arms around me. One hand cupping my butt, his thumb caressing the fissure.

Breathing and panting as we keep kissing.

"This okay . . .?"

His voice is husky. I'm panting harder and harder. He turns his head and kisses the exposed upper swell of one of my breasts, squished against his chest. He licks it and groans and squeezes the flesh, easing his other hand deeper along my ass cheeks to caress my pussy from behind. My clit is squished against his cock. My nipple is absolutely hard and puckered and I feel relief—relief and an intensification of everything at the same time—as he lowers his mouth and sucks me. He sucks me lightly at first, and when I moan, a little harder.

"More than okay," I say, rocking my hips to tease his hard cock, wanting it inside me.

Soon we're fucking, slow and lazy, sitting on the bed, my arms and legs around him, his hands on my ass, moving me, his mouth in control of mine, his hand on my breast, his scent in my nostrils.

I come with a little gasp that he swallows, and he murmurs how sexy I look as he rolls me to my back and finishes off with the most delicious thrusts of my life.

Soon, I start dozing off.

"Come here. I'll let you be the little spoon tonight."

"You been the big spoon often?" I ask groggily.

"Not really but you're so tiny, I could fit in a couple of you right here. Scoot over."

I roll to my side and love the feeling of his arm around me.

I turn to face him and tuck my cheek into his neck instead. I'd always loved being held by my dad and brother, it made me feel safe and protected and cared for. But I'd never been held like this by a lover. It's different. There really is *no* space between bodies. You go the extra few inches closer so that you smell his skin and feel his heartbeat under your cheek —and while you're enjoying that you almost fail to realize he's sort of nuzzling your hair, also enjoying having you this close.

"How many women have you slept with?" I ask.

"If you'd asked me two months ago, I'd say not enough." He groans and shifts on the bed to his back, and I cuddle his side instinctively.

"And now?"

He props himself up on his elbow and looks down at me, eyes thoughtful and intense. "I don't know. It's starting to feel like enough from where I stand."

"As in, you won't want to sleep with anybody ever again?" I laugh. "A man with your libido, there's no way."

"Don't be obtuse, Olivia," he laughs. "No. That's not what I meant. I meant enough to know when I find one who could put all the other experiences behind me."

"Not me, though."

"Why not you?"

"Well, I've got six years to go before I'm twenty-eight. I mean, I want to work a lot and establish myself."

He's silent.

"Callan?"

"Hmm," he says thoughtfully, looking down at me with hot eyes.

"Why are you silent? It's making me nervous."

"Stop talking, Livvy." He sticks his tongue into my mouth, shifting me on top of him to caress me and make me realize he's ready for more.

"So this boss of yours. What does he make you do?"

It's dawn.

We're still in bed.

With a total of thirty minutes of sleep for the night.

We're so fucked.

He lies naked on the bed, slim hips, broad shoulders, the definition of his muscles like a playground under my fingers.

"Aside from sending me to get his coffee twice, sometimes three times because he's too busy to drink it while it's hot, my boss pays me to chew on pencil erasers," I say.

"Waste all the brilliance of that mean little mind?"

"I know, right? *Pfft.*"

He tilts my chin. "I had a good time last night."

I feel a tiny twinge as we part. Is this it? Is this all, and how the other girls end up feeling?

"Am I seeing you again," he asks.

"Excuse me?"

"How's Sunday for you?"

"I . . . um. Sunday is today."

He just smiles at me, waiting.

I laugh and nod. "I might be free Sunday."

"I'll drive you home to change and pick you up at noon? Wear something comfortable."

"Wait. What? Where are we going?"

"Let's do lunch. Maybe some work later. Then dinner."

Butterflies flit in my stomach as he drives me back to my apartment to hurry to get ready for noon. *Okay, Livvy, this is nothing. It's nothing, really.*

But every inch of my well-fucked body knows it's not nothing. The truth is nothing this man gets involved with could ever amount to nothing.

I'm just afraid to know what this something is.

FLAME

onday I have an extra little hop to my step after the fabulous Sunday I spent with Callan.

Mr. Lincoln is back in full swing at the office and he seems pleased with my work.

"In the few weeks I've ever taken off due to illness, I've never come back to the office to find I'm caught up. Good work, Livvy."

"Thank you, Mr. Lincoln."

I dive straight into a set of new proposals he asks of me while he meets with Callan upstairs, and later that same day, I get a message on my office messenger from the CEO himself.

Terrace @ 6 p.m.

I read it over several times and can't help the stupid thudding in my breast.

You know that thing you know that won't do you any good, but you can't stop doing it anyway? It's a little bit like smoking, or getting high, eating too much chocolate, chasing the bad boy. Well that's what Hot Smoker Guy is to me.

I'm beyond wanting to keep a distance now. I can't stop getting close. I'm the millionth woman in the universe who's found her flame and realized she's just this tiny, fragile little moth, helpless to fly away from it.

I work, and work, and work until my alarm rings, signaling that it's six o'clock.

I put my stuff away and lock my drawer, then I take the elevator up with mixed emotions. Mainly excitement, and a little dread for the things I can't help but feel inside me.

I step outside and breathe in the warm summer air. The sun blazes orange on the horizon. I stay clear of the railing but my eyes scan the terrace, side to side, for him.

I spot him in a lounger, checking his phone, a cigarette dangling at the corner of his mouth.

A frisson of electricity runs through me when he senses my presence and lifts his head to look at me, his hair tousling in the wind.

It's hard to remember he is not my Hot Smoker Guy right now.

Hard to remember my name is Olivia stupid Roth.

"Would it be terrible of me to ask for a hit?" I ask him when our eyes meet.

His lips twitch a little higher, and he pries the cigarette out of his mouth and pats his side.

I head over.

I take a seat, take a drag, exhale and pass it over. He looks down at me with a smile, and I smile back.

It's 8 p.m. and we're still on the terrace, with two cigarette stubs in an ashtray on the low table before us when his strong hands circle my waist and lift me to his thigh.

I curl my arms around his shoulders and clutch his hair.

"Not here," I beg, a soft laugh leaving me.

"Olivia," he says even as I kiss his full lips, prompting him to softly kiss me back, "if I'm to make you come for every one of those hundred men who failed to do so, we're going to do this all over the place."

His voice is thick with desire.

"Have you been thinking of this?" he asks.

I bob my head up and down. "I saw you at the cafeteria and I hated everyone for being there, keeping me away."

"One of the interns, I think his name is George, wouldn't stop looking at you."

"What?" I gasp in surprise, and choke out, "I didn't notice."

"I did," he assures me. "Do you want to know something?" He strokes both my nipples over my shirt with his fingers now. I'm wearing a bright pink bra for his benefit and his eyes darken when he notices it through my cream silk shirt. "I used to like it when you taunted me. I'm not that sure I've got it in me to play this game anymore."

My heart starts pounding.

"I want to punch every guy who looks at you for more than five seconds." He cups me between my legs, lips curving. "Because I want more of your sweet, wet little bush."

"Callan!"

"What? Won't you give me more of this sweet little bush?"

"Stop saying that."

He grabs my hips and leans close. "Saying what? Sweet, tight little pussy."

"Don't."

"Your perfect, pink pussy."

"Callan!" I kiss him to shut him up.

"Say it, come on," he huskily croons.

"No, you're having fun with it. If you want my golden little bush . . ." I start laughing.

"God, you make me hot."

"I'm not done," I assure him. I really want to taunt him now.

"You talk about how much you like dick, I'm going to lose it," he warns.

"Dick. Oh yes, I love it."

"You saying naughty things makes me insane."

We're so hot for each other when we arrive at his place. Callan brings out the red scarf I'd worn as a hair band and I tremble head to toe as his touch begins to brush over my skin and my nipples. He wraps my bandana around my eyes.

I can't see him—but this intensifies every touch to the maximum.

Callan turns me around and presses me against the wall. I thrust my butt out as he opens his mouth on the freckles on the back of my shoulder and licks his tongue over them, twirling it over my skin, opening his mouth even wider to suck on my shoulder.

He kicks my legs wider apart. "Make room for me."

I flatten my palms on the wall and turn my head, and he's there, taking my mouth as he drives in.

He's in me—his flesh full and throbbing—and I groan and start slowly dying.

He jams his hand around my waist and between my legs, caressing my clit as he takes up a rhythm.

"How does that feel, Livvy?" he asks. His gruff voice sends pricks of pleasure running through my skin.

I lick my lips, aware of how fast I'm breathing. Of Callan's own deep breaths.

"It feels . . ."

I trail off, no words for it.

WORK AND PLAY

Nobody, *nobody*, knows how to work and play better than Callan.

At Carma, we're all business. But every evening, it's all playtime.

And *I've* become this man's favorite playground.

He's played with me every night for the past two weeks. We usually end up at his place so he can take work calls during the evening, but we've ended up at my place too. We've been bingeing like troglodytes on each other.

I'll say this: Sleeping with the boss is sexy.

Going to work every day for him is sexy. Talking to him about work is sexy. Being taken over by him is sexy.

Even the danger is a little bit sexy.

Except the few times when it's . . . worrisome.

"The only bad thing is that if anyone finds out I'm doing the sexy with you, they're all going to think I got ahead because I slept with you," I told him one night when we were at my place.

"The important thing is that you're going to know that they're right." He touched a finger to the tip of my nose.

"Callan, shuuut it!" I groaned.

He laughed, then shifted over, his big weight on top of me. "Come on, Livvy. You'll have your own business. You and I will be fighting over the market."

"Like Mr. and Mrs. Smith? I kind of don't like that."

"What do you like, huh?" he'd asked, rocking his hips.

The heat in his eyes had stirred awake my every pore, and I'd tilted my pelvis beneath him, nudging his hard cock with my hips.

"That," I breathed.

"Really? You like . . . this?" We were naked. My condom basket had really taken a hit.

He'd given it to me slow at first, teasingly, and then hard, harder, and hardest—and I'd walked into the office the next day with a sore V and a big grin on my face.

That week, when I head up to his office with some papers Mr. Lincoln wanted him to have, I couldn't resist baiting him as he skimmed them.

"I'm disappointed," I said, breathless.

"Explain why you're disappointed," he said, setting the papers down.

Standing next to his chair, I leaned down to his ear. "You're this wicked bad boy, always teasing me. Instead of taking advantage, hugging me and feeling me up, you're being too much the gentleman."

"We're in the office, Miss Roth. Let's not forget we have work to do. Expansion plans for GRT. Plus . . . you've got to get your head in the game. Alcore's wide open." His hand cupped my knee under my skirt and trailed sinuously higher up the back of my thigh.

"But the news is bad on its last quarter," I said, confused and breathing a little hard when his finger started skimming up the back of my leg.

He cupped my butt and sat me on his desk as he took up the papers again and continued skimming. "Sometimes a financially sick corporation with carryovers and write-offs can merge with a healthy one to make big business," he told me.

And I found out he'd just made a tender offer for the company.

Now it's Friday evening, and there's a get-together at Carma to celebrate a milestone. It's an employee- and family-only event. It's well underway when I arrive wearing a low-back silver dress with my hair in a sleek ponytail.

Familiar faces from Carma swarm the party room, and I greet those whom I know and smile at those I don't.

All the time, I keep scanning the room in search of one face in particular.

At the far end, my eyes snag on a tall, dark-clad figure.

My mouth dries up when I see the back of his head. I remember reading *Gone Girl*, how amazed I was by the description of his wife's skull, how well he knew the back of her head. And Callan's skull is the first skull in my life that I seem to know with that same intensity and with such vivid memory. The hair short-cropped at the base of his neck and slightly longer and wavy at the top.

I somehow manage not to stumble as I walk forward, even when I feel his eyes suddenly compulsively rake me head to toe and in between.

Am I still wearing a dress?

Because he's looking at me as if I'm not.

He's dressed in a black suit, and his jacket hugs his shoulders like my arms want to.

I don't, of course.

I spend the night mingling with a drink in my hand, stealing looks and wishing I could just stand there with him.

I catch Callan's gorgeous face canted in my direction nearly every time I let my eyes wander his way.

He doesn't miss a beat in his conversations, but his eyes darken a bit when our gazes clash. We're staring at each other when George taps my shoulder to ask me if I'm okay, why I'm so distracted.

I see Callan's eyes slide to him and his jaw clench, his smile fade as someone whispers something in his ear.

"Oh. I'm great!" I say, pulling my gaze free.

Two minutes later, I head out of the room and into the ladies' room. I look at myself in the mirror; I'm flushed just from being close to him and wanting to be closer. Urgh.

I wash my hands and take a moment, then ease outside just as Callan steps out into the hall.

My heart skips, and we share a smile as I quickly step into a little nook in the corridor.

When he notices I'm blushing, he just chucks my chin and says, "Are you hungry?" Fixing me with a look that makes me even warmer.

"Starved."

His mouth devours mine softly.

"Me too," he whispers, lips curving lightly at the corners.

I'm about to leave when he takes my fingers in his and gives them a little reassuring squeeze. "Meet me out in the car at half past twelve."

"Okay."

We sit through dinner at separate tables, both of us laughing and engaged in conversations while locking gazes, over and over.

The night feels endless until, at twenty before twelve, Callan smiles that toe-curling, smirkish smile and motions toward the doorway. A dull ache thuds in my chest as I set my drink aside, grab my clutch, and tell the other interns I'm beat and heading home.

I refrain from saying that I'm taking the CEO home with me.

The moment I step into his house, his hand leading me inside, he stretches an arm out and shuts the door.

He kisses me, hard. Possessive. Driving his tongue as deep as he wants, his hands massaging my bum as he presses me back against the door.

I pull free and meet his hot gaze. I catch my breath, our eyes holding. I push him back a few steps, past the foyer and to the middle of his living room. Then I lower myself to my knees, and his chest expands as he holds his breath, his eyes on fire.

I take him out and run my tongue over him, watching his face. But it feels so intimate and I'm so engrossed with the hard velvet feel of him and taste of him, I close my eyes and simply suck him, not even for his pleasure but my own selfish one.

I'm dangerously

unashamedly
nymphomaniacally
in love with this big cock.

He shifts and pulls me up to my feet, scooping me up and taking me to the couch. He sits and brings me with him as he stretches on his back—then he flips me around in a 69. He whispers as he kisses the inside of my thigh. "Come on my face. Huh? Do that for me, huh?" He licks deep inside me.

"Oh god, Callan."

"Bend over me."

I take him in my mouth, ramming the thick flesh as far as I can take him. I rock my hips as his tongue works me and I go off in record speed when not only do I feel him tongue me deeply, but also hear him groan as if I'm the most delicious-tasting thing ever. I'm definitely not the most delicious-tasting thing ever.

Because I've got the most delicious-tasting thing ever in *my* mouth.

TALK

didn't sleep one wink and I'm not one bit tired after the orgasms he gave me. I feel amazing, delicious. Also, hungry. And shy.

I'm enjoying my time so much as we have breakfast, coffee and pastries and the most delicious green tea I've ever tasted.

I brazenly stroke my bare toes up his calf beneath the breakfast table as we both read the paper.

I love that Callan's lips curl as if by their own will when I head a little higher, but he doesn't stop reading. It makes me wonder if he reads the paper every morning. Wonder what it would be like to wake up and see him with his sexily mussed hair every morning.

"What are we doing today?"

He eyes me above the top of the paper, eyebrows raised, eyes warm on me as he then folds it. "I don't know about *you*, but I'm doing you."

"Callan!" I groan but blush deliciously all over.

He laughs softly, and then grits his jaw as if he's in pain. "I've been thinking long and hard about this—and I'm talking to Roth tomorrow."

My teacup clatters on the saucer. "What? What do you mean?" When he only sends me a commanding look, I blurt, "You don't need to talk to him . . . This is just between me and you, and it's just a fling. It'll only complica—Look, I'm only here for two more weeks."

"And?"

"And I'm not staying here. You're not looking for anything serious." I pause. "Are you?"

"I'm looking at her."

"You don't mean it. You're fixated on me, like some company you see potential in; the more you think you can have it the more you want it."

"Olivia," he *tsk*s softly, reaching across the table and tugging me around it until I'm on his lap. "You're pleasant company, but you're not a company."

I'm scared to believe him. I don't want him to talk to my brother, I don't want him to pretend this is different, I don't want to expect that much. I just want him.

I just want to binge and binge on him until this ache in my chest goes away. "I don't want to talk."

"Me either." He rubs my ass as I rub his thigh.

"Let's just enjoy this while it lasts, okay?" I beg.

He stares into my eyes. "I want to make it clear I have no shame when it comes to you. No rules I won't break for you. Something about you gets to me like nothing ever has. I say the word *woman*, I think of you. *Female*, I think of you. *Sexy*, I think of you. *Sweet*, I think of you."

"God. Don't be sweet to me. It will just make it harder to leave."

"You want hard? Last night was hard." He looks at me—and I realize he doesn't like our situation. He's not the kind of man to be anyone's dirty little secret. He's the kind of man you flaunt.

And apparently, I'm the kind of girl he'd come clean for.

"I'll tell him when I'm ready," I concede, needing him more than I did a second ago. Something that I thought was impossible.

The steely determination in his eyes softens at my words, and he grabs the back of my neck possessively and pulls me to his devouring mouth. No more talking for now.

DINNER WITH THE GIRLS

I have an enjoyable dinner with the girls that weekend, but I'm dreading telling my brother about Callan and me.

My worst fear now is that Tahoe is going to punch Callan.

I don't want my brother to punch Callan.

I'll punch my brother if that happens.

I feel protective of my guy, even if he's only temporary. Callan not only looks like a bad boy, he acts like one too, and everybody's going to blame him. They're going to act as if this is such a bad thing, when it's not bad. Not at all.

But I'm dying to talk to someone about it.

I'm quiet, sitting here, when all I want is to shout it to the rooftops. But saying it aloud will only bring more complications, and I already know that it's going to end soon. So I only tell the girls that I went to Navy Pier with him recently, which surprises all of them.

"Wow. He invited you?"

"I sort of invited myself." I laugh, then smirk and sip from my straw.

They're dead silent. And then they all seem to talk at the same time.

Rachel tells me you really can't know a guy until you've opened up to each other.

Wynn says even then apparently things that have been buried too deep take a while or a trigger to surface.

Gina tells me to listen to my brother, that he wants what's best for me.

And I just listen and that's that.

CARMA

The next week, Callan's got a thousand things on his plate, it seems. A successful recent acquisition needs restructuring, and Alcore's fighting back against his takeover.

My eyes are blurry at 9 p.m. I'm on my seventh cup of coffee.

I hear the elevator of my floor ting, and I see Callan step out and we smile.

We're the only ones in the building.

"You should be home," he says.

"Not if you're still working," I say stubbornly.

We both start for the elevators.

He smiles approvingly. "You have time to track my schedule?" He absently pushes a part of my loose hair back behind my shoulder. "Thought I'd kept you busy enough."

"You do."

As he exposes my neck and runs his thumb along the curve of my throat, a shiver runs through me. "Not enough, apparently." Callan cups the back of my head and turns me to face him. "I must give you something to do with that extra time of yours."

His eyes are glinting playfully, and I blush and say, tongue in cheek, "Maybe."

His driver, Lou, pulls the Range Rover around the curve as we exit the building.

Callan and I climb inside. We head along the streets of Chicago, Callan quietly staring out the window, a thoughtful expression on his face.

I reach out and take his hand. He doesn't seem to notice, so I squeeze it, silently inviting him to share.

"I'm sorry." He turns, rubbing a hand over his face, squeezing my fingers. "I'm distracted; I'm not on my game." He looks at me with a pause, then adds gruffly under his breath as he eyes me beneath drawn brows, a warning/playful gleam in his eye, "Taking over companies used to be more fun before you made me question everything."

I just stare.

I'm falling for him. I want to say, *Your whole heart for my whole life*.

They say nothing is guaranteed. Except I know I'll never feel for someone the way I do for him. Not for a moment.

What can I do?

"I can sleep at my place—" I offer.

But he cuts me off with a brusque "No."

The look in his eyes when we reach his house is absolutely possessive. Sometimes we stop for dinner. Sometimes we order delivery to his home. Sometimes his chef leaves dinner prepped for us.

Tonight he doesn't seem hungry for anything but me.

Our fingers linked, he leads me to his bedroom.

I want to erase the frustration from his brow and the shadows from his eyes.

"Maybe a part of me feels if I tell my brother, he'll take you away. You won't be just mine; you'll be accused of seducing me when the truth is, I was little nymphy Livvy who—"

He bursts out laughing. "Livvy. I wanted you the second you asked for that first hit."

My breath catches. "Yeah?"

"Yeah." He strokes my cheek, his voice gentle. "Let me handle T. I'll schedule lunch with him. Seems right for me to be the one to tell him. Plus, something tells me you'd apologize, and there's nothing to apologize for." He eyes me intently—my face, my lips, my eyes.

"I just don't know if it's worth it. I have only a little more than a week . . ." I scowl menacingly. "I'm not sure it's worth you getting punched by Tahoe. I happen to be fond of this face." Softly, I reach out and touch his jaw.

His lips curve upward in amusement. "Trust me. You're worth it."

He looks at me for a while, as if something I said touched him deeply. He smiles as he leans his head.

"Come here, Livvy. I've been craving you." His arm slides around my waist, pulling us flush.

His kiss is so very warm. He lowers his head even more and kisses the upper swell of one of my breasts, then moves on to my "freckle," over my top, kissing it, laving it, and it feels amazing.

He draws me up to his length, his hands covering my ass. He squeezes, then clenches me tight in a bear hug as we kiss.

We don't move, only our lips do. My fingers spread on his back and I feel everything, his hands splayed on my back and his chest flattening my breasts. His frame nearly swallows me in a cocoon of muscles and strength and warmth.

He watches me as he strips off my top. He lowers the bra cups and he sucks the peak of one nipple into his mouth. He turns his head and does the same to the other nipple. Then he lifts his gaze, leaving both my nipples wet, the cool air making them pucker even more.

I'm breathing through my mouth, disheveled and out of control as I grab the back of his head and try to pull him up to kiss me. He obliges me with a kiss that turns my toes to full-on tingling, then lowers his head and swipes his tongue over one nipple again, then the other, as he continues unbuttoning my shirt and smooths it off my shoulders and arms.

Then it's gone. I'm in my slacks and bra, and Callan is shirtless and I can't get enough.

He takes my waist, serious about shit now, and flips me around, pressing me up against the wall and kicking my legs apart.

I'm trembling and as turned on as I've ever been in my life.

I shiver under the stroke of one hand on my hair, from the top of my head to my back.

He works off the rest of my clothes and then his, then he runs his hand over the front of my body as his erection teases my ass cheeks from behind. His dark, seductive voice is in my ear. "You're irresistible. I can't keep my eyes off you, my hands off you."

I nod. *Likewise.*

He teases his cock over my folds. I groan and push my ass out, waiting for it.

He thrusts in once. He pulls out. I groan.

He flips me around, lifts me up by the ass and carries me to his bedroom, and I curl my legs around him as he lowers me down on the bed, rolls on a condom and then joins me on his back, dragging me over him. I part my lips, wanton as his tongue strokes mine and I suck and lick and rub his tongue back in a whirl of heat and passion and recklessness. I sit on him—his cock plunging all the way deep with the first thrust.

Oh god, I'm drunk on this.

He's breathing fast, but I'm breathing faster. His hand covers my cheek and holds my jaw. I'm helpless to his kiss, while his arm holds my hip down and he rocks his hips in a powerful motion and fucks me. Like really, truly fucks me, as if he means for this to be the last fuck of his life, or at least mine.

"No more thinking about consequences; there are none. The risk is ours and ours alone—only between us," he repeats.

"Yes," I say.

Though I know this guy is so much more comfortable with risks than I am.

I turn my lips to nip at the heel of his palm, and he releases a sound I'd never heard him make before, like a growl that contains one word inside it—Livvy.

His lips smash to one of my "freckles." Then the other.

I don't think a man has ever kissed me like this, unleashed a hunger like this on me, awakened a hunger like this in me.

We move fast and crazy, rolling on the bed until I straddle him, and when he peels his mouth away from my raw breasts, we lock gazes.

I search his dark eyes, nearly bronze as he looks at me.

He rubs the freckles on my shoulders with his thumbs.

I stroke his jaw, not wanting him to stop thrusting inside me.

Doubts try to trickle in, that I'm getting in too far and deep, but they don't stand a chance against this—against *him*.

He rolls us over and now he's on top, pulling out. Watching me as he drives back in. I groan. He exhales sharply, loving it.

I hadn't realized how much I've grown to need this, how intensely he makes me feel alive, happy, female. Wanted.

And in this moment, it just cannot be wrong, nothing as right as being with him feels could be anything but perfect.

When we're done, I lie on his bed and listen to his breathing.

His nose is at my neck, smelling me.

He strokes my hair from the top of my head to my back.

Once under the covers, his arm comes around my waist, pulling us flush.

I feel relaxed, and so content, tracing the words "I love you" on his chest with my fingertip as my eyes flutter shut. I'm slowly lulled to sleep by the scent of his expensive cologne and a touch—light and tender, almost as if it's alien to a man like him.

FUUUCK

I stir awake to a voice in the distance and Callan's arm slipping out from underneath me.

I stir awake and sit up when I recognize my brother's voice growling, "*Carmichael!*"

My eyes dart around the room in search of my clothes as I watch Callan leap into his slacks and head out of the bedroom, shirtless.

I glance at the clock and realize he missed lunch with my brother.

Oh my god!

Fuck.

Fuuuck!!!

I dress haphazardly and try—really try—not to lose my shit. My whole body is trembling guiltily as I tiptoe down the hall. I can hear Tahoe. His voice is low. Lethal. Furious.

"This is my sister's bag, these are my sister's fucking shoes, this is her fucking ring. You touched my sister? I'm going to break you in two!"

I run over to them. "No!" I cry.

Both men glance my way. Callan's jaw turns to granite as he clenches it. He shoots me a dark and powerful stare, then he puts me behind him and addresses Tahoe in a surprisingly— admirably—calm voice. "I encourage you to make sense in the next few seconds, take the path to the front door, and get out of my home. I'll be happy to discuss this with you—alone."

Tahoe's face is getting redder by the second, the veins popping out of his neck as he charges. "You *mother*—"

"Tahoe, no!" I leap before them, stopping Tahoe in his tracks. Callan shoves me behind him again, his hand clenching my waist harder this time in a silent message that I *stay* there.

A scream of unfairness gets trapped in my throat.

Tahoe glares at me past Callan's shoulder. "Get dressed. We're leaving. Now."

Callan moves forward and I grab him by the shoulders, stopping him. *"Don't,"* I plead in his ear.

There's a tense silence as the men face off.

"You leave with me," Tahoe says warningly, his eyes shooting fire at me again.

I grab my shoes and slip them on and forget about anything else I might be leaving behind—like my damn heart—as I grab my bag and tuck it under my arm, hurrying to leave and get these two away from each other.

"I'll be back," Tahoe warns.

"I'll be waiting," Callan says.

"Olivia." Tahoe rakes his hands through his hair as we head out of Callan's home and toward Tahoe's Hummer in the driveway.

"I love him!" I cry.

"Jesus!"

"I fucking love him!" I climb into the car and once I'm in the passenger seat, I start crying.

He gets behind the wheel and pulls me to him, growling, "He's not what you need."

"He's your friend."

"I wouldn't give him the time of day if I were a girl like you, who wants the things you do."

"I do and I did and I will." I punch his chest.

"What the hell was that for?"

"You're . . . Stop treating me like a baby. I'm a woman! *He* treats me like a woman."

"For how fucking long!"

He glares at me, and suddenly he gets out of the car and charges for the front door. I run after him and my chest literally hurts when I'm back inside and I notice Callan's mega-pissed-off expression as he stares at my brother.

"You're either all in or you get out now," Tahoe says. "Do you hear me? She's not your plaything, she's my *sister*."

"Get out of my face before I break you in half. She's got a mind of her own, and so do I. I might not be what *you* wanted for her, but I'm what she wants and she's what I want."

"For how fucking long?! Tell her that now."

Tahoe shoots off the dare but doesn't even wait for an answer, angrily pulling me back outside.

I cry all the way to my apartment. My brother doesn't say a word. He's stewing. I can feel his anger and his frustration.

But most of all I sense his disappointment and the feeling that I betrayed him.

I've never felt so low.

Callan had wanted to talk to him; I had insisted that I'd do it, but had I meant to? Not really. Now their friendship might be ruined forever.

"Don't hurt him. I was the one who started it," I say stiffly, then I get out of the car to dead silence and peer back inside, mad now. "If you touch him I'm going to hit you, Tahoe! Really *hard*!"

"Oh, I'm gonna hit him," he stews. "I'm going to fucking break his damn nuts!"

I slam the door shut and march up to my apartment, stewing too.

I'm frustrated, wandering restlessly around the apartment, cursing my life and cursing both men and then cursing myself for not telling Tahoe sooner. I keep calling both numbers and neither of them answers. I finally lie down in bed but it takes forever for sleep to claim me.

NEWS

I dream I'm lying on a hill in our Hill Country home, the sun warm to the point I'm almost hot. But there's a breeze rustling by, cooling my skin. I hear footsteps and raise my head, and Nana is there, looking like about a million bucks.

"Nana? You look amazing!" I gasp.

"I feel excellent, Livvy, EXCELLENT!" she says.

She's wearing a big crown on her head. I squint at it. "Where did you get that crown?"

"What do you mean? It's mine. It's always been mine. We're the queens of effing everything, remember?"

She takes it off and comes set it on my head, looking at me with the biggest smile and warmest eyes ever.

I wake up to a knock on the door, and open it to see Tahoe. He looks like shit. He drags a hand over his beard, growls low and painfully, "Grandma passed."

TREE HOUSE

We fly back to Texas in Tahoe's jet, my brother and his copilot at the controls.

In the car, the three of us—he, Gina, and I—are all quiet. My brother has a black eye, and he keeps rubbing it in frustration. Gina keeps her hand on his thigh in silent support. I want to cry but something blocks the tears. *Shock.* I stare out the window as Tahoe drives us to my parents' place, the familiar Hill Country cityscape rolling past us, knowing I won't see Nana again.

"You okay, Liv?" Tahoe asks when we park in my parents' driveway.

I'm silent as I step out of the car.

He grabs my wrist and stops me, looking down at me with brotherly concern.

"You and she were very close. Why aren't you crying?" he asks me, frowning.

"Because I'm mad." I sweep away and head to my parents' home, where Mom and Dad open the door and hug me.

"I'm sorry, Dad," I tell my father, because Nana was his mother, after all. But I can't hold the hug too long, my throat is on fire and my whole body feels as tight as a ball with no way to crack open.

I let go and head up the stairs, straight to my room, and I sit on the edge of the bed and just stare at the ground, wondering if Nana felt any pain, wondering if she was scared, wondering why I wasn't here, wondering why I'm so angry.

I feel numb, robotic after the funeral, receiving a thousand and one hugs, one after the other—*I'm so sorry, our deepest condolences, the world lost someone very special*—and I only nod, and nod, and nod, until I'm engulfed in a pair of familiar arms, and my lungs fill up with the distinctive, addictive smell of Callan Carmichael.

His lower lip is split—right in the middle—and his gaze is the rawest I've ever seen it. A scrape in my heart, that's how the sight of him feels.

We ease apart. His timbre is low and partly questioning. "I didn't like that you didn't come to me. That you didn't let me hold you."

"I had to leave. I couldn't think. But I wanted to."

He gives me a look that implicitly tells me how much he wants to be here for me now. "So are you going to rob me of comforting you now?" he asks me.

"No."

He opens his arms.

I crawl inside and the well in my eyes opens. He's strong and feels warm and so good and he smooths his hand gently down my hair and my back, resting his jaw on the top of my head as I'm tempted to cry for the first time.

He squeezes me tight. "I'm sorry, Livvy."

"I'm sorry too. It's okay—my mom said she didn't suffer, you know."

"But you are."

"Well, we had this thing. I could tell her anything, and she would laugh but not in a mean way, in a loving way, sort of like you do." I sniff. "This wasn't supposed to happen when I wasn't here to even say goodbye."

"You can't plan the bad things that happen. They just do."

The next person in line sort of skims around him and embraces me, and as the line continues, I keep stealing glances, watching him as he hugs each of my family members, counting the times I feel him glance in my direction until I lose count.

Black clothing, bodies, heat, flowers, and food flood my parents' living room hours later, and among all those faces it's only my nana's face that I don't see. People keep talking, their well-meaning *sorrys* invading my brain, everything going fuzzy. For the first time in my life I have been rendered speechless. I'm this numb.

Veronica and Farrah are fawning over Callan during the reception at my parents'.

"Your boss is so gorgeous it's not even slightly hilarious."

"It's like a *GQ* parade here."

"Gina's engagement ring almost poked my eyes out."

"Are you and the boss . . ." Veronica wiggles her brows. I almost wonder if she's asking me if she can go up there and have a go at him.

"Yes," I say. If I sound possessive, it's because I am.

I hear their excited giggles as I stand and walk around a while to avoid any conversation. Callan stands with Saint and my brother. Tahoe hasn't taken his eyes off either of us. Callan is watching me as I head to just sit on a couch thoughtfully. He starts coming over—Tahoe's eyes narrow, but Callan doesn't care.

I get to my feet and cross the room to meet him.

"Olivia," my mother calls to me from across the room, stopping me midway. "Are you okay?"

I nod, feeling a little jolt as I see Callan still approaching. He looks terribly big and terribly strong as he nears me, and he cannot get here fast enough all of a sudden.

"Hey you." His voice is husky.

"Hey you back."

He leans closer. "Why is it you're the most beautiful woman in the world, yet also the loneliest?"

"I'm just . . . processing."

I feel myself sinking into his eyes when my mother—not appeased by my nod—gently draws me aside and scans my features in concern. "I was going to wait to tell you, but maybe you need to know now so you can start processing every-thing." She tucks my hair behind my ear, and I wait in silent dread for whatever it is she looks concerned about mentioning.

"She left a note. She asked me to leave it for you at the tree house."

"What?" I scowl, and suddenly I'm so mad at Nana. For not letting me say goodbye, for leaving me. For dying. I stomp outside. Tahoe had reattached the ladder after stupid Jeremy tore it away, but I never went up there again. Even though my brother built it, someone tampered with it and it's no longer safe in my eyes.

But I feel suicidal, I'm so sad and mad.

I stomp down the yard and head to the tree house, climb up there and then just sit and stare at her handwriting.

I open the letter and tears are falling before I even read the words.

A life of fears is no life.
Live it fully, my Livvy.

"Olivia?"

I lift my head and my eyes well.

"I'm up here!" I call.

I swallow the emotion back and tuck the letter into its envelope when Callan reaches the top.

He looks so out of place in a suit, always so perfect and hot, climbing into the tree house that is so the complete opposite of Carma, I'm torn between laughing and crying because the only reason Callan would be in anything like this would be . . . I guess . . . for me.

He struggles to find a spot next to me and folds his knees to his chest. I show him the note. I look a mess and try to wipe my eyes and right myself as he reads it.

Callan is cramped, his big shoulders hunched as he stretches his feet and pats his thigh. This playhouse was made for kids, not fully grown adults.

He lowers the note and hands it back to me. "What are you afraid of now?"

I shrug.

"What is it?" he asks.

You. My plans not going like I wanted. Losing what I love most.

I settle for a simpler answer. A more immediate one. And just as true. "If I kiss you, that you won't kiss me back. I feel like I'll end up like Jeremy, go down in a tantrum and leave you up here so you never kiss anyone else either."

"*You* kiss *me*?" He lifts a brow, smiling tenderly. There's a sadness in that smile, in both our smiles. Because it's a sad day.

"It's an idea," I defend.

"I have a better idea. Me. Kissing you." He cups my face and kisses my lips softly. I miss him so much, I launch myself at him.

We kiss, and it feels so good to get lost in him and his warm, wet mouth and his slow-moving, gently sucking tongue. I suck a bit too hard, and he groans and I remember his split lip.

When I pull back to breathe, he's smirking.

I touch his lip with my index finger. "I'm sorry about this," I say.

"I'm not." He smiles. "I'm sorry about T's eye."

I frown. "How did that go?"

"Let's see now. He said he would keep it to one punch because you asked him not to hit me. So I kept it to one because he's your brother."

"Thank you."

"You're welcome."

He smiles down at me in tenderness. Then I am pressed to his side, his arm around me, his shoulders hunched over me.

And I realize my new favorite place is inside his hug. No other hug compares. I glance around the wooden house.

"So many years to get back up here. Now I don't want to get down," I admit.

"And this is one place that should send you into a panic." The wood creaks beneath us as he shifts, and he laughs.

"Well, I'm not. I'm with you," I defend myself.

He looks mildly puzzled and sardonic. "I'm no Clark Kent, Olivia. The sooner you know that, the easier it will be."

"Who needs Clark Kent when I have Callan Carmichael?"

"My ego, woman. Stop feeding it." He tweaks my nose. "You think I'm Superman."

"I think you're Henry Cavill as Superman." I grin, and I sit up and admire the way the sunset streaming through the slits in the wood plays on his face. "I don't know what I think you are. Don't even make me analyze it too closely right now. It's just the way I feel when you're near. A little safe and a little breathless and a little happier than when you're not."

He sits back and tugs me close so that I snuggle against his side again. "I, on the other hand, feel crazed when I'm near you, and crazed when I'm not."

"You're never crazed. Only OCD."

He laughs softly and the sound is reassuring. I hadn't realized how exhausted and wound up I was until I feel myself relaxing now.

"I knew my grandma would die. I mean, I knew she wouldn't be with me forever, no matter how much I wanted it. But in my mind, it was after I was twenty-eight, maybe around thirty-five, after she met my husband and my two children one day."

"Two children?" he asks in interest.

"See? You probably don't even like children so you better get out of my fucking tree house now."

"I'm not fucking leaving. Hell, I like it here." He extends his legs out as far as they can go, and his smile fades. "Nobody ever plans for the bad things."

"Every time I lose someone, I get *so* mad. You'd think I'd only be sad. But I get so mad. I'm so selfish."

"You're not selfish, you're hurt. You lost someone you cared for."

He's holding me and it strikes me with painful intensity how I don't want to lose him. I realize it would make me madder than mad to lose him, despite being afraid of loving him because he's not the husband I pictured. He's more, and he challenges me and he keeps me on my toes and pushes me, and also makes me melt and respect and learn, and admire and want him, want him like nothing in this world.

He'll be a difficult and infuriating husband. Hell, he won't even want to be anybody's husband.

I don't want to wait until the timing is right, because it's never going to be right.

I won't want anyone the way I want him.

I never have and I never will and I know it.

I'm pretty sure I'm irrevocably in love with him.

Suddenly I don't want to wait until I'm twenty-eight anymore. I'll be like an old lady by the time I'm twenty-eight. But at least I'll be worldlier, more able to make a decision like that.

"I had a dream the moment she died. Do you think she was saying goodbye?" I ask him with a small scowl.

"I don't know, Livvy."

"But what do you think?"

"What do you think?" he counters.

"That she was saying goodbye."

"Then she was saying goodbye."

Later that evening when the house is near empty, I hear Tahoe and Callan talking out on the patio terrace. Callan sits on a chair, shoulders hunched, hands steepled, and he's breathing deep and slow.

"Don't ruin it. I see the way she is with you," Tahoe says.

Callan drags his hands over his face.

"Look if you're not all in, get out now. My sister has lost enough, she's hurting enough."

Surprise makes me gasp, but thankfully I cover the sound with my hand. Callan drags his hand over the back of his neck, quiet. I nervously wait for a reply.

I don't want him to get out. I want any piece of him I can get.

Quickly, I step outside, letting the door bang loudly as I step out to the porch.

Tahoe doesn't turn to see who it is, but Callan lifts his head as if he can innately sense it's me.

I smile tremulously at him and extend a cup of coffee, just like he likes it.

He looks like he wants to both crush me in his arms and run away from me as fast as he can.

Gina steps out with another bang of the door, and she seems to take in the scene. I guess it's stupid to assume the look I'm giving Callan is only visible to Callan. And the look he's giving me is only visible to me.

It's been a long day, I suppose.

"I have an idea. Why doesn't Callan stay here tonight?" she says brightly. "I can sleep with Livvy, you guys can fight it out over the bed in Tahoe's old room."

Both men laugh as if there's no way they'll fight out anything—both men's egos too big to be in the same space.

"I'll be at the hotel. I need to leave tomorrow anyway." Callan stands and looks at nobody but me.

He leans over and sets a kiss on my cheek, and I curl my fingers into my palm to keep from pushing them into his hair and feeling the warmth of his mouth on mine.

My room is upstairs, and though my parents could probably sleep through the apocalypse, I hear Tahoe and Gina's rough lovemaking. I guess my brother needs the outlet, because they've been at it for a while.

I toss around in bed and everything reminds me of her. Everything makes me crave *him.*

I grab my phone and text him at 12 a.m.

I wanted you to stay.
I'd sleep in the tree house with you.
You're missing out on cramped shoulders and a permanently injured back, boo. :(

My phone rings, and my heart leaps as I see his name on the screen. I answer and hear his voice, husky, though I'm not sure if it's husky due to sleep or something else.

"I'm game if you are."

I lie there and say nothing, praying my brother hasn't scared him away. I don't want to hang up. I whisper, "How about we sleep on the hill just past the house?"

"A night sleeping on a hill?"

I bite my lips, hearing the amusement in his voice. *Please God, don't let what my brother said scare this guy away.* I say, "Yes. With you."

"I'll be there in twenty."

"I'll see you there."

I leap out of the bed and take a quick shower, blow-dry my hair, pull it back into a ponytail, and slip into comfortable sweatpants and one of my sleeping T-shirts.

I leave a note on my pillow just in case Mother peeks into my room.

I simply say, *I'm sleeping on the hill.*

I grab a tote bag and go raid the kitchen, adding water bottles, two blankets, then tiptoe out of the house.

I walk up to the figure on the hill, his shadow making everything inside of me bubble with an odd longing I'd never before felt in my life.

"Hey," I say fake cheerily, "I brought blankets. Two. One so the ants don't get us, another for you and me."

His shoes are next to his wallet and rental car keys and hotel key. He's barefoot. Freshly showered, jeans hanging low on his hips, and a T-shirt that looks so soft and inviting, I want to nuzzle myself into his chest.

I pull out one of the blankets and he takes it from my hand, his eyes meeting mine in the dark before he whips it out and spreads it on the ground.

I sit on it and he drops next to me, the weather too warm to use the extra blanket for now.

We stare at the hills around us. "It makes me humble. Being outside. Nothing man can create can equate to this."

Callan's amused half-smile and the twinkle in his eyes appear. "Well, it took billions of years to become this, scientifically speaking."

I smile. Him and his stats. I don't think he's thinking of stats, though. He leans forward and sets his hand on my back, pulling me close. I absorb the way he smells and the way it feels while we're surrounded by all this stillness, the sights and scents of the woods.

He drags his nose over the back of my ear, scenting the spot where I dabbed perfume. "As far as I'm concerned, there's only you."

It feels so natural, and also primitive.

"They say new, unfamiliar experiences release dopamine in our brains and we feel happy. Am I the unfamiliar to you, Callan?"

"In a way. But you're familiar enough I feel like I've known you my whole life. Wanted you before this life."

Do you want me enough . . . ? I want to ask.

I don't ask it.

I just want to live for this moment without worrying about tomorrow.

He's stroking his hand under my top as if he wants to feel my skin.

I lean a little into him and hook one of my legs over his. His hand spreads wider on my back as he drags his nose down my jaw to nuzzle me. He kisses my cheek, a sweet, almost chaste kiss. I sigh and lean in even closer, wrapping my arms around his neck and tilting my head up to his.

He touches his lips to mine. I'm so still, as still as the stillness around us, disturbed only by a little breeze. But my pulse is fluttering inside me as I let his lips open mine. I swallow back a moan and grip his T-shirt in my fists as I open my mouth a little.

His mouth tastes like mint and coffee and caramel, and his warm tongue strokes mine as if he's never kissed me before.

I moan, and he inhales sharply in response. He holds my face with one hand and kisses me, hot and wet and deep and achingly tender.

His other hand slips under my T-shirt again and his fingers spread wide as if he wants to touch all of my skin, the touch warm and gentle as he rubs his tongue to mine.

He eases back, and I don't know my name.

Olivia. Olivia Roth. Livvy. Is that me?

I look up at him and we are both silent.

His face is surreal in the moonlight. I blink, wondering if it's really Callan gazing at me like this.

He's breathing hard. A muscle starts working in the back of his jaw. His eyes shine with fierce tenderness and some emotion that I can't place. My fingers are still holding fistfuls of his T-shirt, his chest expanding with every breath.

He shuts his eyes and lays his forehead against mine.

We stay this way for a couple of long, exquisite minutes, the air I breathe warm from his breath.

I stand up and pull my shirt over my head, then shuck down my drawstring pants.

Then I'm naked, and lowering to my knees as he sits up on his arms, his eyes heavy-lidded.

His irises have turned to pools of heat and darkness.

"I just want to be close and feel alive," I say as I kneel back down on the blanket.

"Come here." He takes me in his arms and pushes me down on the blanket, beneath him.

He frames my head with his arms folded and he looks down at me with those gold eyes.

We look at each other for a long, long time, until he reaches out his hand and rubs my lips with his thumb.

He's so tenderly looking down at me—*all* of me. Even the boring spots like my neck and my shoulders and my tummy.

My throat feels tight. My vocal cords are tangled with words that I want to say but I'm scared to let out. I want to tell him that I love him, but it would make it even harder to leave Chicago in one week.

I don't want him to be with me for fear of hurting me.

I don't want to do that to him.

And something tells me that, even if he doesn't love me, he cares enough he might do that for me.

So I tell him everything else.

I slip my hand under his T-shirt and am trying not to pant too obviously as I trail my fingers over his abs, teasing the little hairs near his waistband. "This line of hair from here, your belly button, disappearing into the waistband of your boxers. I love it." My voice is breathy as I let my hand tease his erection over the fabric of his jeans, and his voice is rough when he replies.

"I love the ones here." He dips his hand between my legs.

I buck a little.

He clenches his jaw when I do that, then he sits back and fists the fabric at the back of his nape and jerks off his T-shirt with one swift pull. He stands to unbutton and unzip his jeans.

I sit up almost instinctively to nix the distance between us as I watch him strip. Every line of muscle on his body shifts and ripples as he stretches back down to sit next to me.

My heart whacks madly at his nearness again.

Every emotion in my heart feels as if it's squeezed inside there and it hurts to keep it in. It needs *out*.

We're both naked and my skin singes in all the spots our bodies touch.

Callan reaches up to my nape and inserts all five fingers of his hand through my hair, and he holds my head still as he looks into my eyes as if absorbing me—his eyes tracking my features, one by one.

I'm breathless, memorizing how the moonlight kisses his face.

A muscle ticks in the back of his jaw before he presses his lips to my cheek, dragging them down my jaw, my neck, tasting me.

He lowers me down to the blanket.

"So beautiful."

His tongue pushes back in my mouth and I'm disintegrating on the spot. His skin is velvet gold beneath my eager fingers. I can't get enough of the feel of him. The scent of him.

He's lean and athletic, and he looks even more rugged naked, with his hair tousled.

Crickets chirp nearby.

He cups and suckles one of my breasts. I gasp. The tug of his mouth on my nipple makes my back arch.

He parts my legs with one hand, and his fingers caress my inner thighs first. I stroke his jaw and press a kiss on his lips and he rewards me by swirling his tongue inside my mouth as he caresses my folds, gently with two fingers. He teases me with a fingertip.

I feel his fingers slide, first one, then two. Then he's plunging deeper and slower.

"Ohhh. I . . . *Callan*."

He starts kissing a wet path down my abdomen as his hands part my thighs. My eyes widen when he pushes my legs wider apart and then he's tasting me. I gasp and press instinctively up against his mouth as his tongue probes. I moan, and he groans in reply and moves his lips in a hot trail up my abdomen, kissing my nipples again and then my mouth as he eases his fingers back into the place where I most ache.

He takes my breast in his hand and drags his tongue across the tip of my nipple, then covers it with his mouth.

I'm trembling, and he vibrates with urgency.

He looks at me and touches me at the same time, eyes coasting the swells of my breasts to the pink tips, which are puckered to the point of pain as I pant beneath him.

He winds a path with his lips down between my legs again. His hands remain on my breasts; he scrapes his thumbs over the peaks, then there's the heat of his mouth at my sex, and I'm melting, pulling him up by the hair, wanting his weight on top of me and his skin against mine.

I writhe, and he curses softly when he realizes how much I need it, need *him*.

He leans over, and I hear the rustle of his slacks as he pulls out a condom and rolls it onto his hard cock. He leans over me, and I rub my legs against his thick, muscled, hair-dusted calves, then wrap them around his hips. And then he's inside me.

That first thrust feels nearly orgasmic.

We're not speaking.

But suddenly, we're fucking a little wildly and making a lot of noise.

Without the walls to contain them, the noises we make seem to go on forever. Groans and moans as we make love, more like mating, a little animal and a lot hot. His hips rolling and his ass flexing, his back muscles bunching beneath my fingers, my thighs squeezing around his hips, my ankles locked at the small of his back.

"I'm in so deep," he whispers. His hair falls over one eye and I brush it aside.

Adorable.

He's so adorable.

My ruthless Chicago shark in the woods, as natural as if he'd been born here, from the earth, and me too.

"So fucking deep," he grits out as he grabs my head and crushes my lips with his, never stopping his kiss, never stopping the rhythm, until I'm unraveling between him and the warm blanket beneath me.

We lie there sated for a little while, not even covered by the extra blanket. Our skin looks radiant in the moonlight, sweaty too.

He draws me to his side and brushes my hair back, then strokes his hand absently over my shoulder as he asks me, "You okay?"

Maybe it was the intense lovemaking, the intense emotions of the day, but something in me breaks loose, and I start crying from one second to the next.

He moans as if it pains him to see me cry and I bury my face in the nook of his arm, feeling him squeeze me. "You'll be okay," he promises, his lips buried in my hair and moving against my scalp.

"Yes," I say, nodding, amazed by how much I needed to cry, how much I am not trying to stop crying because it just feels right to cry in his arms.

I didn't bring tissues and just when I start to try to dry my face, he holds me by the jaw and licks up my tears, even the ones that trickled down my neck.

I clutch his hair and kiss the top of his head as his warm tongue laps me up, turning my feelings back to desire rather than loss, love rather than grief.

"Are you really going back tomorrow?" I ask him.

"I have to."

I swallow. "Would you mind if I stayed a few days? I just want to support Mom and Dad."

"Take as long as you need."

"I will. Not too long. Otherwise it'll be time for me to get back here again," I say.

The thought of the end of my internship and my time in Chicago feels a bit like a mood killer. The thought of a ticking clock on my time with Callan is also an aphrodisiac, and I'm determined to binge on him before I leave, just like I can tell—by the way he starts kissing me and ravaging my body hungri-ly—that he's determined to binge on me, too.

ONWARD

I visit Nana at the cemetery every day for the next few days. I am mad and sad and guilty and more. "I always thought I would be able to talk to you when I fell in love, Nana. Now what do I do?"

The next day I ask her, "Should I tell him I love him?"

The last day, "If I should tell him I love him, send me a sign."

I hear rustling behind me, glance up at a tall oak to spot two squirrels fucking.

"What is that supposed to mean? Really, Nana!"

I'm mad again as I pack my bags, then I just want Chicago. It's not that I love the city any more than I love Texas, but it's what's in it that I crave most.

Strange how homesick I was for Chicago. I hadn't realized how much until I'm back and feel the warm wind in my face

when I step out of the cab and I walk into my apartment building. I hadn't told anyone I was on my way back. I even booked
a ticket on a commercial airline and flew—on my own. I vom-
ited only on takeoff and landing. I call that a small victory.

He's the first one I call. I get voicemail, so I leave a message.

"Hey. I'm back. Just wanted to say hello. Call me later."

He immediately texts me.

In NY
meeting
couldn't pick up.
Back around 2 a.m.
When are you getting in?

**I'm in! Left you a message. Though I'm probably
turning in earlier than 2 tonight. I might be too tired to
hear the door. See you tomorrow?**

Looking forward to tomorrow
Miss Roth

Oh, Mr. Carmichael, you know, so am I.

I'm smiling when I lower my phone, but my smile soon
fades when I think of how soon I'll be leaving again for good.

Wynn's the second one I call, because she left a thousand
and one messages on my phone, apologizing for not being able
to come to the funeral. The moment I tell her I'm in town, she
tells me she's coming over.

They say good friends never ask if they can come over, they just do.

It makes me happy to have found one in Wynn.

"Sorry about your grandma," she says the moment she steps into my apartment and gives me a huge hug. "I had a gallery opening of a new artist, I couldn't get away, everything was falling apart. My thoughts and prayers were with you. Are you okay?" she says as she pulls back to study me.

"Yes. And you?"

"Okay."

"You look pretty. Where are you going?" I ask, eyeing her soft blue strapless dress.

"To have dinner at Emmett's restaurant," she confides.

"Oh! Did he finally—"

"Oh no! He doesn't know I'm coming." She grins, but her eyes look sad. "Maybe he'll join me. Maybe he'll just see me and . . . I don't know. We can finally talk things out."

"You're not going alone." Before she can protest, I head into my closet to change into a swirly black skirt and a black top. I still don't feel like wearing colors, even though I know Nana would want me to.

Thirty minutes later, Wynn and I are at Emmett's newest haute-cuisine restaurant, called Pear. I'm so famished, I could lick my plates dry—the food is phenomenal—but Wynn hardly takes a bite. She keeps glancing around the restaurant. My heart hurts for her because she's trying not to make it seem like she's looking around.

We ask for the check, and there's still no sight of Emmett. The waiter sets it down on the table and says, "The tab is taken care of."

"I . . . oh, well thanks," Wynn says, breathless. "Can I say thank you to the chef?"

"He's terribly busy." Obviously the fact that he doesn't even hesitate means he was already given instructions not to allow this to happen.

My heart now aches for Wynn, but Wynn won't have it.

Her eyebrows crease into an angry little frown as she signals at the spot where her plate had been resting minutes ago. "Well, see, I wanted to complain about the undercooked duck."

I widen my eyes and barely keep from saying, *You hardly ate the duck, and it was so good!*

"I'm sorry, miss. I'd be happy to take your complaints to him."

Wynn's eyes spark in even hotter anger and she sets her napkin down. "Thank you, but since I don't plan on returning, that's quite all right."

We head outside and start walking in silence.

Wynn is stewing.

I have no real clue about relationships—the only one I've had really has no definition at all. An affair. A fling. It'll be over in days, once I finish my internship, and so what advice can I possibly give Wynn?

I stick with the usual. That if he doesn't come back, or fight for her, or at least try, then he just doesn't deserve her.

I worry about Callan and me. I worry about it hurting. Better to pull out right now than be hurt like this—

"He's such a fucking—Do you know he just one day pulled back? One day, said he just didn't want kids even when we'd talked about it before, when he'd asked me to move in —"

"WYNN!"

We hear a male voice yell behind us.

Wynn and I both spin around at the same time.

Emmett stands there in his chef jacket.

I wait for Wynn to do something, but she just kind of stands there and does nothing but stare.

"Fucking come back here, Wynn." Emmett starts walking for her and I nudge Wynn.

"Go on!" I hiss, and Wynn starts walking cautiously forward, and I turn away when I see him grab her by the front of her dress and pull her in for a kiss.

Well then!

Grinning ear to ear, I pull up my Uber application and call a car, then head back to my apartment.

I don't sleep.

I'm counting the seconds until tomorrow when I see him at Carma.

I've only got a few more days of my internship. Staying in Texas sort of took up my last week—it's killing me to know our seconds are counted.

FAREWELL

I'm planning to be at the terrace at 6 p.m. sharp today.

I really wish I had time to look up Callan sooner, but I can't.

I'm trying to get as much done for Mr. Lincoln before I leave. My fingers are flying over the keyboard when there's a dramatic shift of energy in the air around me.

I glance up from my computer and he's leaning on my desk.

Hot.

Unattainable.

And so sexy he sends me out of my goddamn mind.

Callan.

My Callan.

Our gazes hold each other silent.

My mouth starts running dry.

"I've been told I'm a selfish bastard." His lips hike up mockingly. "Never really realized that I was, until I caught myself wanting to call you a dozen times, asking you to come back home."

"I *was* home," I croak.

"Yeah, that's right." He laughs. His warm eyes are full of expectation. He looks almost perfect, but the slightly disheveled imperfections—including the tousled hair and dark circles under his eyes—I find adorable. Adorable enough that I could reach out and grab it, anchor myself to him.

"How are you?"

I fiddle with my sleeve, looking at the keyboard in front of me. "Good. There's so much to do though to get ready to leave."

His gaze swirls with some raw, dark emotion, and he says, "I'll leave you to it, then. Come home with me tonight."

I nod eagerly. "After that thing at the Saints'," I say.

He grabs my face and kisses my cheek and I close my eyes and groan and drop it to the desk.

That night, my brother's gang throws a farewell party for me.

Wynn picks me up and tells me she and Emmett are working on things.

"He thinks we're moving too fast. He's not ready for kids," she says, sighing. "I'm willing to give him time, you know? I believe in us."

I'm envious of Wynn, of how sure she is that they can work out. When right now I just don't even know what I want anymore. My plan had been so crystal clear when I came to Chicago, and now . . .

My breath catches when we stride into the Saints' penthouse apartment. Because he is the first thing I see.

He's wearing this puzzled expression as he stares down at a gorgeous, chubby, black-haired baby, as if he can't believe he's holding one. Then he flashes a smile at it and tells Saint something that makes Saint nod proudly.

Seeing him hold the baby does something to me.

He's still smiling as he shoots a glance in my direction.

It seems like a casual glance, as if he doesn't know I'm standing here. But he finds me staring and when our eyes lock, his gaze shines a little brighter, his smile fading. He crooks his finger at me and points daringly at the baby.

I shake my head, just to be contrary.

"Come here, Olivia," he dares, nodding at the baby. "Don't be a coward," he croons.

"I'm not a coward. Having one of my own is in my plan, but I bet it's not in yours."

I sigh and relent.

Callan waits for me to come over—fuck, but he looks so hot with a baby in his arms—and when he hands Baby Saint over, he smells of my favorite Callan cologne, and the baby smells like baby, and our hands brush as he passes him over to me.

I sense a shift in him when he gazes down at me as I hold the baby.

Is he thinking of getting me pregnant?

Of having his baby girl or boy in my arms?

"Stop looking at me like that, Callan." I shoot him the direst warning look that I can.

"Like what?" he asks, his expression still intense and un-changing.

"You know what! It only makes me want it, want *you* to—" I catch myself and give him a telling look that clearly states I don't want to want these things, then I finish off the look with a haughty lift of my chin as I turn around to take the baby over to the girls.

"Hand him over!" Wynn says, and she sits him on her lap and kisses his cheek.

I steal a look at Callan for only a tiny moment, seeing the familiar twist of amusement dancing at the corner of his mouth.

Ask me to come tonight, I think as our gazes hold.

But really what for?

If you touch me tonight, it'll only make it harder to leave.

Already seeing him with a baby in his arms makes me want it to be my baby that he's holding—his and mine.

I wish it were that simple.

I had my whole life planned out, and maybe Callan won't change his spots for a girl—there's a reason he's the last man standing.

Wynn offered to drive me back, and being at the Saints with Callan so close and yet so far away was eating up my nerves. I could sense Tahoe watching us when Callan and I stepped outside to smoke.

He brushed his fingers over mine every time we passed the cigarette, and I wanted to hold his hand, kiss his lips.

We didn't talk. That's *so* unlike us. Callan seemed frustrated by the attention we were getting, and he spent the evening nursing a whiskey and smoking more than usual. He noticed me leaving with Wynn, and he caught up with me at the elevators.

"Olivia?" His voice stopped me before boarding. "You're coming home with me."

I flushed when I noticed Wynn's eyes widen. I glanced nervously at the group where my brother was, grateful he wasn't looking in our direction. "I'll stop by later," I quickly said, to appease him.

Callan looked at Wynn then as he dug out his car keys from his jeans, as if planning to leave now himself. "Give her a ride to my place?" he asked her.

Wynn looked at him as if seeing him with new eyes. She had eyes only for him as she nodded. "She'll be there."

"Good." Callan glanced meaningfully in my direction, then told Wynn, "Give me a head start," and so Wynn and I lingered for a few minutes before we finally took off.

"You love him?" Wynn asked as she drove me to his place.

"Yes," was all I said.

She smiled privately, as if she knew something I didn't.

Now, I'm walking into Callan's home.

I close my eyes and tell myself to breathe. I almost walk back and leave, but I swear to god something keeps me where I am. And yet I can't move forward.

I marvel at the fierce tug of emotions that brought me here to him in the first place. I want so bad to reach out to him and let him hold me but I'm scared that if I do, everything will change.

I'm scared that if I take this step, and walk toward him, and let him hold me tonight, I won't be the same in the morning.

I won't be the same ever again.

I walk forward, my shoes soundless on the modern rug, and the hair on the back of my neck tingles with anticipation. I can hear my heart beating so fast and so strong I'm scared he'll hear it, that he'll know.

The door of his office is open. I part it wider and spot him at the far end. A bottle of whiskey and an empty glass sit on the desk before him. He looks incredibly warm, his huge body taking up most of the space.

He stands. "I knew you'd come." Callan meets me halfway across the room and cups my neck, and the slow stroke of his thumb there sends shivers down my spine.

"You asked me to."

"Sit here."

He guides me to sit on the desk and as I climb on, he draws my hair clip off my hair, pushing the loose tendrils aside as he leans his head forward, and my breathing hitches with the feel of his lips touching mine.

"I'm desperate for you." His fingers trail up my thigh, under the fall of my skirt.

I moan. "Callan."

"God, I come unglued when you make that sound."

"Callan . . . We really have to stop at some point."

His hunger blazes in his eyes. "I haven't slept since Texas. Not seeing you every day . . . I feel crazed over you. Unhinged. I'm insane for you." He tugs me to the edge of the desk. "Come here. I can't wait." He spreads my hair aside and kisses the curve between my neck and shoulder. Tingles race down the line of my spine, down every vertebra and nerve ending.

I moan again.

"I'm a reasonable man. So why, when it comes to you, do I have no reason?" He rubs my lips with the pad of his thumb. "I have no control when it comes to you. God, look at you." He tugs my shirt open with a flick of his fingers over my buttons. He pries it over my shoulders and swoops down to cradle my lace-cupped breasts and kiss the tips over my bra.

My body is wound up with desire and yearning. "Callan, this will only make leaving more difficult . . ."

I'm trembling, yet even as I watch Callan strip with fast jerks of his wrist on the drawstring pants and T-shirt he's wearing, I can't bring myself to stop him.

I know I can break. I know this can break me. But I could never feel as broken as I will when I'm alone, staring up at the ceiling, remembering his touch and wondering if I will ever feel it again.

I reach out as he reaches for me, and I kiss him.

I have the first good night's sleep I've had for days.

God. Loving this man has been both the easiest and the most challenging thing I've ever done.

I want to be that girl who finds love and just takes it.

But what about my career?

I want to be his equal. I eventually want to know as much as him, do as much as him.

I can't help thinking that if this were happening like I'd planned, at twenty-freaking-fucking-eight, I wouldn't have to choose.

I want to stay.

But it'll kill me not to pursue my career dreams too.

I stay with him for longer than I should, prolonging the time in his arms.

When I'm sure he's asleep, I kiss his jaw and inhale him, wrapping my arms around him as tight as they will go. I tingle when he reciprocates, loving the way his arm clenches me even as he sleeps, then force myself to let go.

"I love you," I whisper in his ear and steal away, without looking back.

And every step away from him feels painful.

LAST CIGARETTE

I spend all day organizing everything for my departure.

Callan spends all day in board meetings.

His assistant has returned from maternity leave and Janine has been boasting how eager she is to apply for a permanent position at Carma, now that her internship is over. Like her, I'm officially done with my summer internship. When the clock strikes 6 p.m., I have my stuff in boxes.

And when I head upstairs at six and Callan opens his office door and leans on it, simply looking at me, I feel a stirring of longing so deep, I almost whimper. I feel like one last cigarette with him.

I NEED one last cigarette with him. Fuck the seven minutes of life it takes from me, life *is* that terrace and him and me.

He seems to read my mind, because he shuts the door behind him and motions to the elevators.

Once we go upstairs, we're silent for a while. Not even smoking. Just sitting there in silence—and for a while, it's enough. Breathing close to him, listening to his breath. Occasionally stealing looks and soaking up the sensuality of his physique. I'm so attuned to him, I'm painfully aware of every breath he takes, of how deeply he inhales, exhales, how warm his body temp is, where his eyes are focused.

And they are on me.

He studies my lips briefly, and I can't help but drop my gaze to his mouth, which looks full and firm. And I want to kiss it again. I want to feel it all over me again, full and firm but also soft and warm and hungry times a thousand.

I don't know how I'm going to do it.

How I can say goodbye.

I think of Texas and my hope for a future business, trying to make this moment less painful. It'll be exciting, but it won't be as exciting doing it alone. I then decide I'll take a job until I'm ready to go it alone, and someday I will ask my brother to invite me over for a weekend in Chicago, and I will look Callan up and hopefully I won't feel this squeezing in my heart. And at twenty-eight, I'll be ready to meet the one who wants the same things I do and . . . well, wants to be together. Officially.

I tell myself all this, and yet my heart doesn't buy it.

It feels as if I'm leaving my red bandana knotted around the railing, flapping aimlessly in the wind because I'm too afraid to reach out for it, and nobody is helping me. And I never asked him to help me.

Callan lights up and hands me the cigarette, looking at my mouth with acute intensity as I take a hit.

"We should stop smoking," I say, exhaling.

His lips quirk. "Okay." His eyes are crowded with something beyond lust, beyond anything I've ever seen in them before.

"Really?" I ask, passing him the cigarette.

"Yeah. I've been keeping it to one a day, two. When I'm not talking to you." He grins, his eyes pools of warmth and swirling heat.

"Really, wow. Then we should definitely stop smoking," I say more firmly. Maybe my reasons are also the fact that every cigarette will remind me of him, and I'm not sure I can deal with the pain of missing him that having one will bring.

"We should," he concurs.

"I'll do it for my nana."

"I'll do it for you."

My skin tingles, and a sudden warmth engulfs my core. Is this one of his antics? He looks so somber now.

"Let's do it then," I say with forced cheer. "Report back at the one-month mark."

"Sounds good."

I smile and let go of a breath I hadn't realized I'd been holding. It seemed to be trapped in my chest. But now I breathe a little easier, after this deal we made. It's better this way. I get an excuse to talk to him. It doesn't feel like such a final goodbye. I can't take it otherwise.

"Wynn and Emmett seem to have gotten back together."

"Did they?"

"Yes. I mean, I don't know the details. I'm sure she'll share soon. But I'm happy they could work it out. All this time, I've been thinking about relationships. How sometimes chemistry and attraction and compatibility are not the only important things. Goals are, too. If you're here, and he's there, well . . . he's not where you are."

"People can move. From here to there. I can move, Livvy." He looks at me quietly and smirks. "I can move faster than anyone."

"Call me when I'm twenty-eight," I plead.

He laughs, and then he falls somber again.

"So we're talking of you being unable to be the one to come from there . . . to here?" he asks me.

"I don't know. I suppose . . . we can figure it out. It's not like we can't talk sometimes."

"Agreed."

"It's complicated. I mean . . ." Can we simplify? How about we simplify? "Maybe when I'm twenty-eight, you'll be ready, and I'll be ready too—"

I'm waffling. I know I'm waffling.

"I'm just going to kiss you for the hundredth time, if that's all right with you?"

His finger slides up my cheek as he cups my face in his palm and presses his lips to mine, and my toes curl a thousand and one times. My heart beats a thousand and one times in one second.

I'm panting when he pulls back to look at me with hot hazel eyes.

"I'm going to miss kissing you."

He looks at me. Just that.

Just looks at me.

My throat is tight and I cannot, cannot, breathe. I want to tell him to tell me to stay. I want to tell him I love him. I want him to tell me he loves me back. But I'm afraid. Afraid that this is just a moment, that it'll pass.

That he'll leave me. That I'll leave him.

That it just won't work.

Stop being afraid. Just trust in this, Livvy.

I lift my head and kiss him and he groans softly, licking my lips. He pulls my face closer and licks me again, a deep, tender flick of his tongue.

Then his lips are gone and I'm silenced by his dark, thoughtful expression.

"I was always going to go. That's the plan, right? Own a business at twenty-six, etcetera etcetera," I say.

He looks at me. "Letting you go right now is the most un-selfish thing I've ever done."

"You're the one who gave me the courage to really believe I can follow my dreams and do it."

He just looks at me, his eyes really dark.

My eyes sting.

"Goodbye, Callan. I . . . I learned a lot."

And I did. I learned you can't always count on your life plans to go your way. Sometimes some higher power somewhere has a bigger picture. Puts you where you didn't expect to be. To learn what you need to learn. Life sometimes doesn't run in the cycles it's expected to. We are all here for a blink. Life changes in a blink. We fall in love, sometimes, in a blink.

He stands and clenches his jaw, shoving his hands into his pockets. "It's a stupid rule, Livvy. So are some of mine. We like to control our environments, but the more I try to control this, the more it slips out of my hands. Time doesn't matter, really. I understand you have your rules, but I'm breaking yours when you've done nothing to break mine."

"What?" I ask, laughing.

"Just saying," he says. There's a warning in his eyes.

"Goodbye, Drake."

"Goodbye, Fanny."

I take my promise ring and put it in his palm. "Can I give you this? Not like a promise or anything, just . . . I don't know," I ramble. I kiss his jaw and force his palm closed around my ring. "Goodbye, Callan."

I hold it together as I take the elevator to the lobby and head home with my box. But I fall apart with my grandma's queen of everything pillow.

I don't feel like a queen now, I don't feel like anything amazing now.

Tahoe drives me to the airport.

I'm hiding my weepy, swollen eyes behind a pair of sunglasses, quietly staring out at Chicago.

"Carmichael came to talk to me."

I think I hear my heartbeat faltering. "Oh."

"He talk to you yet?" He seems very curious.

"No. I mean, we said goodbye yesterday. We're friends and on good terms. We're texting each other next month if he manages to stop smoking."

A silence, then a soft chuckle. "Okay then. Call me and tell me how that goes."

I don't know how my brother can sound so amused when I'm sure that I won't feel amusement or true joy for a long time in my life again.

"You going to be okay?" he asks as I step out of the car and Tahoe comes around to hug me.

"Yes." I look into his blue eyes, so like mine. "Don't get into any fights." I scowl at the fading bruise around his left eye.

"Don't make me," he warns, then he grins and wraps me

in a bear hug. "You tell him you love him?" he asks.

I shake my head. "No. It's better this way. I don't want to pressure him into anything and I belong in Texas."

"Do you?" is all he asks, his lips half curled even as I nod emphatically and board his plane.

I feel an odd sense of loss. I smile and wipe a tear from my eye and clutch my vomit bag as I fly in my brother's jet back to Texas, though the feeling in my stomach doesn't seem to be related to my fear of heights at all.

I just don't know if I'm flying in the right direction.

This was the plan. Callan just wasn't in it and now that he is, I'm struggling to believe what my nana once said, that maybe I could have both. I'm transported to the terrace. *Olivia. Callan.* To his teasing smile. His expectant gaze when he pushed me. To the way he lost control in bed. To the cigarettes we shared. The stolen looks and the forbidden touches and the talks.

The talks.

The slow, irrefutable, irresistible smile of his. It was perfect.

He was perfect.

ALL IN

Callan

Lovely girl.

Lovely fucking infuriating girl.

She's a fucking lovely infuriating girl and I'm behind my office desk, staring at her fake ring, rich beyond measure and as miserable as they come. My whole life is as fake as this ring Livvy wore.

Jesus.

I let her go.

Despite every inch of me screaming to grab her to me and never let her leave. I could see her begging me to let her go. This is her dream. I won't hold her back.

That's what I keep telling myself.

I'm not fucking buying it, not even for a dime.

I'm not this guy. I'm the guy who wouldn't get it. Why my friends would go balls deep for just one. I do now. This is me now.

I call T.

"I'm all in."

I hang up then I grab my keys. First thing on my mind—a meeting at Carma for some much-needed restructuring. Second, I'm getting a real ring to replace the damn fake one on her finger.

I'll give her a month. But that's all she's getting. I'm not taking no for an answer. This is my girl—all that's required is for the stubborn, irresistible little Miss Roth to see it.

PLAN

Livvy

've heard it too many times. Be careful what you wish for. But still millions of people are out there wishing. I got my wish. I got a kick-ass internship, a kick-ass recommendation from Callan Carmichael, CEO of Carma Inc., and Daniel Radisson scooped me up like a football for the touchdown.

It should feel absolutely great—I'm climbing the ladder of success, step by step.

I could think Callan's recommendation might have been influenced by my bed skills, but I know that man too well: he wouldn't endorse anything or put his signature on any paper that he didn't fully believe in.

And he fully believed in me, right from the start—he gave me a shot. Taught me the ropes. He even let me go so I could chase this dream.

The satisfaction I should feel isn't there, though, because somewhere along the way I started thinking of other possibilities for my life. I should be proud I stuck with the plan. Instead

I feel like there's this giant vacuum in my life and nothing can fill it.

Radisson Investments in Austin wasn't as exciting as I thought it would be. Even with me living with Mom and Dad only an hour away and Nana's grave so close, I'm not as motivated. Daniel leaves me alone and just says, "Good job." Always "Good job." I wonder if he'd say that even if I were putting in only a halfhearted effort. I almost am.

I crave Callan's voice telling me, "You can do better."

I'm thinking of veering off on my own a little earlier than expected, but I know I've yet to sharpen up my investing skills a little more.

Daniel isn't a corporate raider. He couldn't pull it off if he tried. After working at the massive Carma headquarters in Chicago, I feel like the smaller offices of Radisson—no uniform, casual, easygoing surroundings—really don't inspire me to step up my game and get sharp.

It doesn't help that I heard about the Alcore deal. Callan once again surprised me—he holds majority now but allowed the previous stockholders to retain their seats on the board and a larger percentage of stock, and he's injecting capital for an expansion that will take Alcore to the next level—one where millions of sales will become billions. The debt will grow, temporarily, but only until the huge new deals with high-tech companies start bearing fruit.

I applied for a real job, at Carma. I don't feel at home here anymore, even though my parents are amazing and I love seeing my friends. What I got in Chicago may not have been what I wanted for myself. I realize now that life gave me better, so much more than I imagined. I fell in love in a way I never thought I could. I never thought I could have both a career and *him*. I want nothing less.

Fuck the plan, it's not what I want anymore.

I want Chicago and I want for the hottest man in Chicago to be as crazy about me as I am about him.

My new plan is: *Do anything for career* except *give up the man you love.*

I keep refreshing my email all day. It's been a week since I submitted my application, but I've received nothing yet. I'm even considering calling Tahoe but maybe Callan doesn't want me there anymore. I'm home after a full day of work and refresh my calendar to verify it's a month mark. I want a cigarette. I really do.

Me: Month mark tomorrow. Did you make it? I almost didn't. YOU?! Did you stay away?

Him: Hardest thing I've ever done. I'm ready to cave in.

Me: Me too. I'd have one if I had any. I'm too lazy to get some.

Him: I got you.

Me: Haha. Please do. I'm waiting. Make it fast.

Him: Fast enough for you?

I don't understand the message until I see movement on the front porch as I walk up to the house. Standing before me is a vision—a complete hallucination—of Callan in jeans and a black crewneck T-shirt that clings to his muscles and has him looking his hottest.

He's only a few feet away—instead of a whole bunch of states away. And he's hot, amazing, right fucking *here*—his jaw a little shadowed by stubble, his hair rumpled by the wind—and he's never looked as real.

As adorable.

As bad-boy sexy and as fucking *good*.

I swallow the lump that seems to immediately well up in my throat.

I want to sprint to him, climb him like my tree house, and move into him as my permanent home.

I want to crawl on him and touch him all over, kiss him all over. My fingers itch at my sides and my mouth dries up. I feel the attraction crackling between us. The air around him is testosterone-laden and my whole body feels it, senses it. I see it in his eyes as he looks at me the way he used to—with a touch of amusement, and a whole lot of interest, and just a gleam of admiration too.

"Callan," I gulp.

"Olivia."

His voice, oh god.

Oh god oh god.

It sparks up a sea of tiny goose bumps across my arms and I laugh at my own reaction, marveling at his effect on me—always his effect on me—and I tuck a strand of hair be-hind my ear with a shaking hand.

I'm shaking all over as I walk up to my front porch, catching my breath when the air I breathe begins to smell of his cologne.

I take a seat, and he sits beside me.

"Thanks to your recommendation, I got the job at Raddison."

He shifts to his elbows, looking at me intensely, his lips hiking up at the corners. "That's a pity."

I'm surprised by his comment. "Huh? Why?" I scowl at him.

"I'm opening a new division at Carma. I'm allocating a percentage of our investment funds to partner with small, struggling companies. I wanted you as head."

I blink.

I draw my eyes away.

"I couldn't take the chance of you saying no—so I gave you some time." He takes my chin. "I *can't* take a chance of you saying no."

I'm blown away by the offer. I'm blown away by the way Callan is looking at me now, as if I'm exactly what he's been looking for, for a long, long time. "There are other people who can do that job a thousand times better," I whisper.

"I doubt that."

He holds my gaze.

Love doesn't lie. Everything I've never known I wanted, I see in his eyes. It's taken time for me to look past my fears and my plans, and now here he is. Here I am.

"Whatever you want to do, do it now—there are no guaranteed tomorrows, Olivia," he says, jaw clenched as he looks at me.

"Life goes by in a blink, Livvy. Here we are, trying to make sense of it. Stop thinking and just live it. I don't want another second without you. Not one." He shakes his head, then pauses and takes my chin again, leaning closer. His voice drops to a low, deep rumble. "I once told you I didn't know if I could love anyone deeply. I can and I do. More than I ever thought I could."

I'm speechless. For the first time in my life, really. Everything I never knew I wanted sits next to me in six-feet-plus of muscle and man. My friend and my mentor and my lover and my . . . love.

"I told you I loved you," he says, softly, when I don't respond.

My voice sounds soft as cotton. "I remember. You just said it."

"Any chance I'll ever hear you say it back?"

I nod frantically fast, trying to find my voice.

"Climb the terrace we've built and come to the edge, and take a look, Olivia. I'm standing right there."

I croak out, clenching my fingers into my palm, "What are you doing standing there?"

"Waiting for you, you adorable, infuriating, irresistible girl." He thinks about it, then laughs as if at himself, then eyes me meaningfully. "I want you pregnant with my children. I want your DNA permanently woven with mine."

He waits. Then . . .

"Remember when I told you the worst things are never planned?" he asks. "In my case, I think it's the best things in my life I never planned. I never thought I'd own my own business one day. I never planned for my friends, Saint and Roth. I never planned for my brother. You are one of those things. *The* thing. I never planned for you in my life, Olivia," he says, watching me. "I guess you can say I had a thousand small business plans, never a personal one. You know me. I don't like leaving things to chance." His lips quirk a little in amusement. "It always felt too iffy. For twenty-eight years, I was proven right not to have planned for it. But then, there was this lovely little blonde on the terrace of Carma, and she asked me for a hit, and I wanted all of her like I'd never wanted anything. Those wide, scared eyes, that mouth running away from you."

I'm melting and yet I'm still sitting here but I don't even know how. I feel so much love that it suddenly infuses every pore of my body and enlivens every particle and atom of my being.

If I was strong enough to fall for him—for a man like him —I'm strong enough to be with him. He won't be easy. And the realization that I don't want him to be, that the challenge excites me, brings out the best in me, fills me with excitement and relief.

"I don't want you to work for me, Livvy. I want you to be my partner in every way, in every sense. I want to plan good things with you. A future with you. And I'll ride it even if some things don't go our way; all I know is that I want all of it with you. You make it better. You make *me* better." He cups my face and squeezes gently as he looks into my eyes. "I've fallen so deeply in love with you I'm drowning here. I'm fucking drowning here." He shakes his head. "I blinked my eyes and you were gone. It went by so fast, I don't want to blink a second time and find you gone again, not for a second."

I take his jaw and press my lips to his. He groans and grabs the back of my head, angling it so he can kiss me harder.

"I wanted to stay," I breathe as I rain loving pecks on his mouth. "I wanted to say I loved you and I was afraid."

"Say it," he gruffly commands.

"*I love you.* You fucked up my plan and I'm glad you did." I laugh when his lips hike up at the corners and his hand clenches convulsively around the back of my head. Callan couldn't look prouder if he'd taken over the *galaxy.* "It's the first time I've said it to your face. It feels good to tell you."

He stands and lifts me, his hands on my ass, anchoring me to him. "I brought you something." He shifts me on his thigh and reaches into his back pocket.

He hands me a box of cigarettes, and a melty sensation runs along my spine. I open it and, to my disappointment, there's nothing inside. "What kind of gift is this?" I complain.

I turn it upside down, as if magically a cigarette will appear, and out falls a heavy diamond ring onto the center of my palm.

I'm in shock. All I'd asked for was a cigarette. Really. Just a smoke.

"I'm all in," he whispers, looking down at me, his eyes brilliant with happiness as he tips my chin up. "Are you?"

My throat starts closing as he takes the ring and slides it onto my finger. The perfect fit. "This one's as real as it gets." He taps the huge emerald-cut diamond in its center.

I've had flutters, palpitations, and weird feelings in my heart since I met him, but the leaps my heart is doing now have no precedent! "You're going at warp speed, Callan, I . . ."

"You wanted a nudge, this is more than a nudge. I'm taking control of our futures. I want everything. Are you in?"

I clench my lips together and spread my palms on his hard jaw, cupping the face of my Hot Smoker Guy in a way that tells him I'm never, ever letting him go. "I'm in. I'm *all* in."

He strokes his fingers through my hair as he plants a hard, fierce kiss on my earlobe.

I press closer to him. I'm smiling so hard my face hurts. "I'm crazy in love with you."

He's smiling too. His hands like vises around me. "Because you're a crazy girl. Half mad, really."

"Mad for *you*," I counter.

He leans over and captures my lower lip with his, then nibbles on my top one. "Back at you."

I flick my tongue out and taste him. God, I'd missed his taste so much. "Come upstairs with me. No one's home. It's too hot to go out to the hill," I say.

I take his hand and tug him inside, and upstairs, to my bedroom.

I shut the door behind me and head to the bed, looking at him wantonly. "You with your reputation for womanizing, are you sure you'll have enough with me?"

He walks forward. "Got my hands full with you."

"Good, because I'm too stubborn to let anyone else have you."

"No one has me, but I'm having all of *you*," he says, grabbing me and pulling me to him.

"I get nothing? That's not a fair trade." I scowl.

"A little bit of me. This, though?" he says softly as he touches my lips. "I'm definitely having this." His eyes heat up as he lowers his hand and cups my pussy. "Definitely this." His voice gets gruffer by the second as the heat in his eyes swirls around me in a sea of bronze. He touches my eyes with two fingers. "These. I'll take both of these." Then, he spreads his hand on my forehead. "I'm taking this too." He brushes his fingers over my breast, my left breast, right over my heart. "This. Most of all."

"And in return, I get . . .?" I prod.

"An eye for an eye, like they say."

"My whole heart for your whole life?" I dare him.

"We'll see. I want a bonus."

"Like what? I'm giving you everything!" I cry, laughing.

"Like . . ."—he tugs the sleeve of my top downward to expose the back of my shoulder, pressing his smiling lips against my skin—"this cluster of freckles."

I groan.

Shivery.

That's how he makes me feel.

He kisses the back of my shoulder and I tilt my head, enjoying the feel of his lips on my skin as my chest swells.

When he lifts his head and our gazes meet, I'm done playing around.

I love the playful sensuality in his eyes—like he doesn't take anything too seriously. Except maybe sex with me right now. Because there, right under the playful sensuality, is the heat of a thousand suns trained on me. I can't even breathe.

I'm wearing this guy's ring, on my finger. He loves me and I love him.

He's panting as his eyes give me a quiet command to get naked.

I unzip my slacks and shove them off, on a mission, not able to get naked fast enough, then I stare at him, delicious and stunning as he unbuttons his jeans, and his beautiful cock stands out. Callan takes it and strokes, watching me, and I lean over and kiss the tip, then open my mouth, taking everything I can, the whole shaft. He groans.

I shiver.

"Fuuuck." He lifts me in the air, then throws me on the bed. He doesn't even remove my panties, he tugs them aside until they're hooked to the side by my swollen labia, and then he slides into the slick depths of my body. I clench reflexively; we groan from the pulsing, lung-stopping pleasure. My head falls back, my body arching with sensations.

"Oh god!"

My pussy is so tight, his dick so big, he's almost tapping my heart every time he hits deep and I love it. We both do. We're having steady, noisy, out-of-this-world sex and I won't last another minute.

I cry out and squeeze my thighs around his hips, tightening my vagina around his shaft, locking him in. He groans.

He thrusts inside me, his mouth on mine, his body as relentless as mine is, neither of us letting the other breathe, or think, or stop.

This is an avalanche of ravaging desire, his need telling me beyond words how much he wants me.

My orgasm thunders through me. My skin melts; I fly away, ecstasy ripping through me. "Callan," I moan.

He groans in pleasure, saying, "God, I love you," against my mouth as he rides his own orgasm, fucking me through it.

Seconds—or maybe a year—later, I realize my nails are biting into his back and I'm gasping for breath. He's throbbing inside my pussy, still impaling me. I groan and nibble on his neck, loving the feel of him. All in.

"Does this mean we won't have one last cigarette?" I ask, kissing his neck.

"I got a new pack. Somewhere." He smirks as he edges away, then goes to clean up. When he returns, he pushes the window open and brings a fresh pack.

I sit up in bed as he lights a cigarette. I memorize his movements. His hand cupping the flame, his lips pressing down on the end, his inhale, how he plucks the cigarette out of his mouth and offers it to me, his eyes shining as if he's giving me the world.

"Sometimes, on a special occasion, we could have one," I hedge. I already miss this.

"Yeah, we could. If we wanted to."

"Yes, if we want to. I do."

"I do too."

He pries the cigarette off my lips, takes a drag, then passes it back to me as he slides his arm around me, and we lie in my bed and have our last cigarette.

Or so we think.

HOME

Mom and Dad are stoked about the engagement. We spend the weekend with them and before heading back, Callan and I visit Nana's grave.

After a tearful farewell with my happy but jealous friends, on Monday, I'm all packed and ready to move permanently to Chicago.

I'm in Callan's arms, looking out the plane window at Chicago. My new home.

TWENTY-EIGHT

Callan

Six years and a couple of packs of Marlboros later (what can I say, we're addicts), we're expecting. Olivia Carmichael. Fun and sweet girl. Expecting a Callan Junior.

I could spend days listing the things Livvy's done at Carma. We're breaking the rules. Always.

Fridays are Easy Fridays—the Carma troops wear whatever the fuck they want.

But what matters, really, are the things my wife has brought to me. Before her, I never wanted to be better or worthy of a single thing. You don't need to be worthy of what you own if you can afford it. But the love of your girl . . . that's something a man needs to own.

She has a new plan for herself this year. The year she turns twenty-eight.

She wanted it to be a milestone.

It's the year she becomes a mother.

I tweak her nipple and turn my head to her stomach and I kiss it. She's been sleeping like crazy, and I've never done more work from the bed than I have these past six months. Weekends are all about my wife lying around, recharging that simmering energy of hers, while she naps with her head on my thigh, listening to me do my thing.

She asked for a hit that first day on my terrace. But I was the one who got punched in the chest. The Carma uniform had never looked better.

I reach out for my pack at the memory, take out a cigarette, then remember I told her I'm quitting because she has. Not good for the baby, after all. I shove it back down and toss the pack way in the back of the nightstand drawer. I'm keeping my word. I'll quit smoking. But I'm never quitting her.

Watching her walk away all those years ago has been the hardest thing I've ever done. Every instinct of mine demanded I chase after her, bring her back where she belongs—with me.

I opted to be patient. Give her space. Cross my *i*'s, dot my *t*'s—that's the way I work, after all.

She'd have time to think, follow up on her plan.

Except she never counted on that plan encountering a glitch.

That's right, her fucking Drake—Derek, Henrietto—is not waiting until she's twenty-fucking-eight. I spent years playing the field, not interested, refusing to feel trapped.

I'm trapped and I've never felt so fucking free.

I love my lovely fucking infuriating girl.

I'm all in. Every day.

They say you're never truly wealthy until you have something money can't buy.

I wake up to that something every morning. Blonde hair, long lines, loving eyes. I'm the wealthiest man alive.

DEAR READERS,

Thanks so much for picking up WOMANIZER. I'm hoping Wynn will soon tell me her story, as well as Callan's mysterious gambler brother.

As always, and from the bottom of my heart...

Thank you for your support and enthusiasm for this series and my work. :)

XOXO,

Katy

ACKNOWLEDGMENTS

I am so lucky to be surrounded by such an amazing team of people who motivate and inspire me. A very special thank you to my bestie, Monica Murphy. For your friendship, enthusiasm, support, and for the long calls and the short messages and the frequent emails. Most of all, for being just plain wonderful and inspiring all the time. Not to mention, thank you for the privilege of reading your babies before anyone else does, just like you do mine. Here's to many more, bestie.

To my family; I am able to do what I love thanks to *you*. I adore you.

Thank you to my agent, Amy Tannenbaum, who is everything wonderful and more, and everyone at the Jane Rotrosen Agency (more wonderful!).

To my super editor, Kelli Collins, and the fabulous Ryn Hughes, CeCe Carroll,

Lisa Wolff, Anita Saunders, my proofreader, and Angie McKeon.

Also, Nina Grinstead and the entire fabulous team at Social Butterfly PR.

My author friends, Monica, Emma, Kristy, and Kim. And Gel, thank you!

Thank you to my fabulous audio publisher, S&S Audio, and to my foreign publishers for translating my stories so that they can be read across the world.

To Julie at JT Formatting, and my cover designer James at Bookfly Covers, you both did an amazing job!

To Melissa, you know a thousand reasons why.

And to all of the bloggers out there, thank you for all the times you've shared the love and cuddled up with one of my books.

Most of all, to my readers,

your readership, support, and love of my stories and characters means more than I can ever say. Thank you for spending time in our world. :)

Katy

ABOUT

New York Times, USA Today, and *Wall Street Journal* bestselling author Katy Evans is the author of the Real and Manwhore series. She lives with her husband, two kids, and their beloved dogs. To find out more about her or her books, visit her pages. She'd love to hear from you.

Website: www.katyevans.net
Facebook: https://www.facebook.com/AuthorKatyEvans
Twitter: @authorkatyevans

Sign up for Katy's newsletter:
http://www.katyevans.net/newsletter/

OTHER TITLES BY KATY EVANS

CPSIA information can be obtained
at www.ICGtesting.com
Printed in the USA
LVOW11s1815250517
535838LV00003B/605/P